Penguin Books
City of Women

Born in Sydney, David Ireland has lived in many
places and worked in a variety of occupations.
He now lives in Sydney and writes full time.
After some verse and play writing, he turned to
novels. Three of his novels have won the Miles
Franklin Award: *The Unknown Industrial Prisoner*
in 1971, *The Glass Canoe* in 1976 and *A Woman of
the Future* in 1980.

A NOVEL BY

DAVID IRELAND

CITY OF WOMEN

PENGUIN BOOKS

Penguin Books Australia Ltd,
487 Maroondah Highway, P.O. Box 257
Ringwood, Victoria, 3134, Australia
Penguin Books Ltd,
Harmondsworth, Middlesex, England
Penguin Books,
40 West 23rd Street, New York, N.Y. 10010, U.S.A.
Penguin Books Canada Limited,
2801 John Street, Markham, Ontario, Canada
Penguin Books (N.Z.) Ltd,
182-190 Wairau Road, Auckland 10, New Zealand

Originally published in Australia by Allen Lane, 1981
Published by Penguin Books Australia, 1981
Reprinted 1983, 1986

Offset from the Allen Lane edition

Made and printed in Great Britain by
Cox & Wyman Ltd, Reading

CIP

Ireland, David, 1927-
City of women.

First published: Melbourne: Allen Lane, 1981.
ISBN 0 14 005821 4.

I. Title.

A823'.3

The Lost Engineer

My engineer is lost to me, my whole life gone down the drain. Both engineers; our years together — such happiness, such endless wilful days: the travel, the wanderings, the distant jobs — it seems like another country. She'll never be back.

There was no time factor in our love, no tomorrow, though forever was assumed. And the word 'yesterday' was missing; but that was filed away, in memory.

She worked with me on water management systems, assessing valleys, harbours, catchments, breakwaters, lake capacity, tidal flow, water tables: I was proud of her and all we had in common. Ambitious for her, too. Now she's gone, out on her own: a consultant, being a success. Laughing at me. 'Failure's the last refuge of the meek,' she said. In her eyes, someone no longer working has failed, broken down — but isn't that exactly what I taught her? — and the meek have no shadow.

She'll never come back, she's so proud. She even took her dog, Madly.

Do I really resemble a devout oyster when I'm asleep?

She left her old self here, along with everything I am and am not; she's travelling towards what she will be: I have no more changes to make. I wanted everything to stop, just like Faust did: it was perfect. She was my home; now my home is in my head; why can't I be content with that?

I'm old now. Forcibly retired from Water Management Systems, Engineering Division. I gave them so many of their good ideas, things that are procedures now, but they've taken everything I did: methods, data, my work on weather patterning and artesian capacity — captured the lot on a few miniature products of Silicon Valley. Now they don't need me, implied I was lucky to be kept on for the final few years. In view of past achievements . . . and so on.

Sixty-two and afraid of solitude. Deathly afraid.

More than ever I yearn to have a younger person with me, no matter how ruthless. A companion full of life. Bobbie was that to me and I loved her. In her I had found the face I dreamed years before. When I was with her I was in an aboriginal dream valley, unspoiled. She said I was a woman congealed by habit, and called me the Empress Coagula. She came to me with no past but my hopes; I should have been more wary. Instead, it excited me. She left without warning, to dare the omnivorous planet: gave me her breakneck smile, went out to get milk, called her dog after her, and didn't come back. At the time I thought she'd just gone to water down her categoricals.

She loved me once. (I must be here, in case she *does* come back. I mustn't move from this spot.) She used to dream of finding a key to something submerged — the dream always ended with her opening the door to another galaxy. This is one dream I learned by heart.

Billie and Bobbie we were, but to her I represented the Age of Antiquarius.

Bobbie and Billie. She loved dancing.

She thinks that by going, the world will come to her. When she's my age she'll know that without looking out of the window you can see all the way to heaven.

She'd begun to talk to me vaguely, her mind on other things. Stung, when it persisted, I called her Vaguely Vaguely. She shrugged, accused me of being an old sorrybottom. I was alarmed, thinking she'd gone cold on me, beginning to turn her incalculable back.

When I tackled her about it, 'You're heading in the right direction,' she said, 'but your wheels are gone.' And laughed at my thoughts. She knew very well what made me tic.

Now Billie Shockley is lonely in the City of Women, writing letters to old addresses. And Bobbie chose our lady of dollars. No, that's not fair.

Q: When will I stop this mindless mockery and be at least serious about my own pain?

A: I can't. It's part of me. My weapons are my enemies. Fiddling about with words gets to be a habit of the lonely mind, as it clenches and unclenches, grasping nothing.

∽

Far down below the surface we lived, once. We were the deepsea people. Our roof was the interface between the pressure of caressing water and the dangers of empty air. The storms of the ordinary world didn't reach down there, only gentle currents rocking us. We were enclosed, then — together.

∽

By the gargantuan gums of God, I'm lonely! Though I have a new Bobbie whose warm breath comforts me a little, who nuzzles me with affection. I take her round on a lead — my partner, my pard, my pard de leon, my leopard. My new Bobbie doesn't accuse me of being emotionally too involved with chocolates, or being capable of only modified rapture. Or having three chances of happiness: fat, slim and Buckley's.

I must admit, though, she gets my letters and answers them promptly enough, considering. I write at least once a day. She's on the far north coast lately, busy on problems with tidal electric works. She writes on an average of once a month — three weeks, when I'm lucky. Without meaning to, I remember whole chunks of her letters; some things she says echo and echo in my mind; they are so much Bobbie they punctuate my thoughts. Her words have life, to me.

I remember my father, when he left me his word-collection, saying, 'In the beginning was the word. Hang on to words, words can arrange your life, words were invented to arrange our lives. You can name your own days . . .'

⌦

This morning I feel all over the place like a mad man's breakfast; bits of me everywhere; my consciousness, if you call it that, scattered like bits of broken mirror. What happened last night? Suffering Sappho, I can't remember. Did I join the Church of Christ Culinary? The Church of Toast? What's that slight memory I have of telling a group of people I was working on a book, compiling the statistics of pain? Or was I talking to myself — aloud — as I find myself doing more and more?

Apart from my drinking (I intend to control it in the future) I've tried to be as noble a person as I can, and Bobbie was a fair child. Is a fair child. Her integrity rings like a bell. Loves chips and crunching numbers, and endless landscapes with water. Hardly a black mark against her. Her only fault — she sang every time she was sad, and so was I. She called for her meals on a slide trombone named McCoy. (Why did she say I was the surreal McCoy? What did she mean?) I wish I'd never made that remark about bitterly cold buttocks and chilly nipples. Or that unfunny joke about the bargaining position. Such trivial things then, so bitter now.

I remember she used to wake and say she dreamed of feeling sculptures against her during the night.

When I wanted us to get our heads together over possible problems, she said 'We're a long way from Tipperary'; when I asked was there a hitch in our relationship, she observed that 'the eternal verities are all very well but watch the mundane realities'; when I enquired what it was that was unsatisfactory, she replied 'Chastity begins at home'; when I demanded to know what it was I was doing wrong, she said she had 'selective affinities', I was 'feigning sanity', and 'A problem that can be described is not *the* problem.' I begged her to tell me in what way I'd changed. She answered: 'Change changes change.' And turned up her blonde music.

'What can I change in me to stop you not loving me?' I pleaded desperately. It was a mistake. She didn't hear me; she was singing — tunelessly, but it didn't matter — with the music. She sings, and kisses, with a wet mouth. I wish I hadn't pleaded.

∽

When I feel a little better I'll get out her most recent letters. I daresay I'll pore over them for hours before I start writing to her, telling her (more than she wants to know) of my life here, trying to keep out anything that sounds like whining, trying to avoid the word 'alone'. In practice, that means talking as little as possible about me. I don't always succeed.

∽

Do you ever get up in the morning full of energy, ideas, enthusiasm, determined to bend your difficulties to the shape you want, improve your standing in your own eyes, to buck up generally? Ready to tear the living fangs off the world? Then find as the day wears away that the world is indirect, there are no borders to reality; words, objects, thoughts, have only a diaphanous existence; there is opposition to your every effort, including opposition from your self, and the opposition is hard as quartz or so yielding and elusive that you end up flailing the air and in the evening your enthusiasm is gone and you go to bed saying 'What's the use?' Or you go looking for company to cheer you up.

You probably do. I did yesterday. And the day before. Nothing recedes like success.

I'd been down to Cathedral Street where my favourite watering hole is, and came home on the shoulders of four hefty heroines, a little insobrious.

Insobrious? Yes, damn it! Insobrious. The holy bottle left me full as a fart. Each of the four, clad in recessive jeans (there I go again) had a corner of my platform. They provide it for me on public occasions when I've wandered too far into drink: a square of board on which I sit cross-legged as on a magic carpet, singing, beating time to music only I can hear, or addressing a multitude that seems to have gone home. The four bear me up and down stairs, along streets, an eye-catching procession, and deposit me on my bed and leave me to sleep it off. My new Bobbie won't attack female callers.

When I wake, the pictures that form behind my eyelids! The pressure on my head!

As our procession swung off William Street, up Yurong, I was roaring out:

> 'Bums, bellies and tits
> bums, bellies and tits
> nothing so pleasing
> as constantly squeezing
> bums, bellies and tits'

With a few refrains of 'Glory, glory, halitosis' thrown in for good measure. I'm addicted to heroines.

I daresay they're used to me. I did a few years of Medicine at university before switching to Engineering, and they call me Doc. Everyone and her dog calls me Doc. (Does that make me, too, a middleman between the drug company scientist and the sick?) When I visit them they like to show off their ailments.

Yesterday, Wanda Hinckley, one of my classmates in Politics years ago, was beaten up in a disco and crawled home to City Tatts to die. On the doorstep. Didn't even make it inside. The few strollers in Pitt Street didn't offer help. The stone horse on the parapet didn't notice. Wanda's face forms now in the brown colouring I see on my closed lids. Her face changes, as faces always do in my hangovers. Dear Fuckadilla. Always threatening to spend her life writing the history of geography. Hadn't seen her for years; suddenly she comes home dead. I was Fingerella then, until I rose in rank to Cunticula. The times we had. No holes barred.

Roaring, fit to wake the dead.

Wanda had a child, a simple child. When it was nine it began to pray, every day, for the death of the rich. Please kill all rich people and all rich children for Jesus sake amen. And an expression of uncontrollable sweetness. Wanda hated it. She was

5

a social ethics observer, then. Suffered from incipient knee strangles.

Dear Fuckadilla Wanda, I never knew you. No character is ever established. Everyone is different this time, different from last time, and as well, makes seemingly quantum jumps to another state after absence or a night's sleep. Your face comes back to me as it was when we were young, is overlaid with lines until it is the lined mask you presented on the club doorstep, and I confess I shuddered. I still think of my own face as it was when I was twenty, in spite of the evidence. There it is, shining and new, under the wrinkling, ghostly, insubstantial present.

⌒

Out of my window (now I'm sitting up) I look across to the brown cathedral, the deep green foliage of the Sydney Domain, below me to the school, across again to the steel-blue harbour, the pastel colours of Woolloomooloo terraces. It's a Corot morning. Near me, in the triangle of Cook Park and Remembrance Garden, they planted Moreton Bay figs, plane trees, poplars, camphorlaurels — and palms, would you believe? Not a hazy, grey-green and silver-dusted eucalypt in sight, just three white box trees in William Street near the bus stop. No, it's changing, the outlines move and cross each other; it's not Corot and quietness (I don't deserve that), it's Kandinsky, more like — a fantastic scribble, an Op Art puzzle, a Bridget Riley, an eye-twister.

The morning-after regularly wipes the floor with me, doesn't it? Let's make a fight of it, just the same. Give me people! Renoir cheeks, Rubens bums! Less green, less foliage. Nothing happens. Failure. No laughter by request. If I drink like a fish, why can't it be a freshwater fish?

All I see moving are three barefoot runaway girls going east and two derelict women west on William Street, and an old tramp woman sleeping on newspapers on a bench in the sun in Remembrance Garden. Disorder, decay, ruins: Lowry people. Oh, and one girl with a black shopping bag, in a floral dress with a lot of white, talking to herself, coming down Boomerang Street past the orange phone box. What an attractive walk.

Where's Bobbie? Where do you come from, Bobbie darling? She has no way of telling me. Did you come a long way? Escape from a circus? Swim from Timor? The January night you came I was lonely and stayed in and was overjoyed at your scratch on the door.

You took me out of myself. I wasn't frightened of you even then. I gave you meat but you weren't hungry. Had you eaten? I wonder what you'd eaten. You understand me, don't you? If only she could talk, but she listens to everything I say. Of course she understands me. Perhaps it's better I don't know what she ate.

Then she settled down on her rug, good as gold.

I wonder if she's dreaming of the leopard in the bookshop window. Yesterday, I showed her a stuffed, standing leopard in a display for a wildlife book promotion. Life size. That's the closest she's been to leopard company: like me, she's the odd one out. (I can't stop myself.)

Did I leave you asleep in your room last night? Yes, I did. I wonder, did you go out foraging? Did you go to the Edge of the City, looking for men? (Men are meat in the City of Women.) Did you go to the Edge?

Bobbie lies on her rug, lifts only her head as I stroke her. The characteristic leopard smell always has me asking does she need a bath. I don't think so. There's a sort of sweat comes from her flesh and travels out to the tips of her fur, a greasy feeling on her coat.

I often think sweat is the faintest tincture of shit. I wonder.

As I try to eat some cereal I am distracted by the sight of two women jogging over Art Gallery Road past the stone women and the swings. One is heavily built. Two buses, equally heavily built, travelling together — from loneliness, no doubt — wait to swing round the corner from William into Yurong Street. My left tit feels cold. I look down: it drips milk. My food-stained breasts have been dipping into my plate.

'So you've got mouths too?' I say to them. I wipe milk from the left one and from its associate remove two soggy cornflakes. Everything is coming in twos.

Downstairs, the Duke, a middle-aged Corgi of sociable inclinations, formidable intelligence — and a dear person — is barking in a highly critical tone. He barks a bit, then pauses for breath, for he's overweight. He rarely barks; someone must be tormenting him, someone with a razor's sense of fun.

My mind feels like an airy, fragile and extremely valuable cardboard box.

I lift the plate, drinking the rest of the milk. Way down under my window the girls begin to play and yell in the grammar school.

I wonder where she is now? How long will it take her to find out that the further she goes the less she knows? But how can the young be wise enough to know that?

I take down a bundle of her letters. There's her dear hand-writing. How she used to bend her head forward when she wrote, her hair falling round her face, making a little cave within her bent arms. I wonder how she looks at this moment.

> My engineer is a sunrise;
> No one person may have her:
> The sunrise loves no one.
> My eyes prickle when I remember
> Her awkward songs.

A call for the lift registers with a loud click in the lift well, the lift moves in its shaft with a despairing groan (no other words will do) which becomes a steady machine-noise until the lift cage stops somewhere in the building with a minor crash. Four bangs follow as its two doors are opened by hand and carelessly slammed shut.

This lift is sick. Its attendants come weekly, but what they fix allows other symptoms to blossom. It's a permanent invalid, so ill that lift-riders have stopped writing graffiti on its walls: if it stops between floors, there they are — caught with their fresh phrases and shiny words down.

◯

My dearest darling Bobbie, I am writing to tell you about some of the people who live round about. The sun is pouring in — I have abolished curtains. The solemn city buildings look as if they will stand forever; pigeons ridge the roof of the Museum; the gold of Centrepoint gleams; the sun rests on the right shoulder of the Opera House's western shell; the grass of the Domain is succulently green; the sky over North Head is light and clear of cloud and so empty; the sun is everywhere.

The Lover's Arms

Ivy the publican owns Chez Ivy, the Lover's Arms and the Conqueror's Arms, all three of them in Cathedral Street. The Lover's Arms is where I usually find myself, and by eleven, when I took Bobbie out on her lead, Ivy was in the bar phoning for a mechanic to fix the television. I knew she hoped the mechanic would be Linda, a strong young girl of around 175 centimetres and fifty-odd kilos. Arms like ferry-ropes, coarse fair hairs and all. When she's thinking, she widens her eyes and they look just over your head. Bobbie's look down.

Ivy has a sign over the main register 'The buck stops here'. When I feel like it, I call her Dead Shot, refusing to acknowledge the pun she intends, insisting on my own.

Old Georgina was sitting in her corner already, her Siamese cat tethered on a lead looped over the metal rung of her stool. As I glanced at the cat I noticed the shine of a flea's back as it came to the light then plunged down towards the pink flesh out of sight. 'Hi, Georgina! How's it going?' I called. We touched eyes. Hers were bright, brimming with moisture but tired in the way an old dog's are. Mine — but what could I know of mine?

'Hullo Doc,' she answered. 'Doing the best I can.' She knew I loved that answer. She'll be eighty-six in November. She'd been a proof-reader for publishers and country newspapers until nearly seventy; now she was sitting out her retirement in comfort. Since the cat was with her she'd only stay a while, then go home for lunch and come back at five without the cat and stay till nine, drinking slowly. She wrote a book once, *The Young Person's Guide to the Orgasm*, but she never talks about it.

Bobbie treated the cat gently, but the cat retreated in terror under Georgina's stool. I wish people wouldn't think Bobbie is aggressive simply because of her jaws. Animals that eat other animals *look* aggressive because of their dental equipment, but she's not aggressive in herself. Even when Bobbie sees the red woman in Riley Street — red dress, red hair, red shoes — with her white fantail pigeon on a lead, she restrains herself.

'The hunters of youth are about,' commented Ivy in my direction, 'in this surface paradise they call Australia.' In the City of

Women the female is the symbol of youth and the future. The old order was male, and sterile.

'More casualties?' I asked. I loved her once, or thought I did. But what I thought I saw in her was just a shadow of the love I've lost. Anyway, cheer up! Love's a cannibal: when it's eaten another it feeds on itself. And when it's all gone, it's all gone. Until another meal appears. (But what would I know about it? Only that some tears are sweet, *and* salt.)

'Helen Svenssen.'

'Holy powers of piss!' I apostrophised. 'Poor old thing.' Helen was one of Ivy's friends, a giant escaped from a circus that had her under a twenty-year contract. She was the standard giant: a face like a bunch of toes, but a gentle person. With her size and strength she could afford to be mild and never in a hurry, never bad-tempered, always pleasant. She had a peculiarity — a passing fad had stuck to her mind and had impressed on her the living nature of all things; plants and animals. She wouldn't kill, wouldn't even cut up meat when she helped out in Ivy's lunch bar. It was cruel to kill; she would even refuse to cut up spinach.

'Why spinach?' I questioned once. She cut potatoes with a hard enough heart.

'Can't you hear it when the knife cuts it?'

'You give me the pip,' I replied. 'Of course I can't hear anything.' I stroked Bobbie, feeling her fine fur under my fingers.

I remember that day the wind was from the north-east and every time someone opened the door of the pub the smell of the sea came in and invaded my mind. (The sea, the sea! I should have been a sailor.)

Helen had taken to drink. Not a bad drunk — just went home and passed out peaceably — but she looked alarming when she began to weave and stagger, singing 'My best friend is a graveyard'. She often fell over.

She'd begun to get depressed; depression was taken seriously in the City of Women. If she hadn't been so huge, she'd have looked like the classic dying duck in a thunderstorm when she was down.

'Where was it, Dead Shot?' I pursued.

'Darling Harbour way,' Ivy grated at me, while glowering at the bar-girl, who interrupted: 'Why do I have to do it all by myself?' Her supervisor was away.

'She's gone on a personnel management course, like I told you.'

'Just to control me?' squeaked the girl in rising tones. Like a lot of the young these days she was nasty, brutish and tall.

'Shut up and do your work or I'll clip you over the ear.'

The girl grumbled 'You'll get your corner,' but got on with it. Ivy was very fierce still. She'd been a hard doer when she was young; they said she used to suck four guys dry before breakfast.

The north-easter breathed in again at the door, so gentle. The sort of breeze that has the shivery grass trembling on its elegant stems. I do love those fragile grasses; I wonder if I'll ever see them again out in the suburbs.

'Is Helen dead?' I returned to the subject.

'Not yet. I think she will. By the way, that animal trainer I told you about — the adherent of the Marxist confession — reckons your Bobbie would be about seventeen if she was human. You know what I mean, the equivalent in human age.'

'Thanks. Yes, I thought she might not be full grown.'

'They could hardly miss her, I suppose,' Ivy went on, of Helen. 'They got her dead centre, fair in the guts. Some bastard came up like creeping Jesus and potted her.' And she went on with her work. It was only a small number of males who took to violence against us, the rest were glad enough to keep away.

When I'd got my heart started with a Scotch I patted Bobbie and listened to a conversation between the recalcitrant bar-girl and a customer lady who propositioned her. The bar-girl's reply consisted of a twenty-five-word sentence, each word of which was No. The customer's face was one of those you meet that are hard as the hobs of hell. I didn't blame the girl.

I thought of my first Bobbie and our mornings and how undressing her was like peeling fruit; when she was naked I was sure she looked more appetising dressed: dressed, I thought the opposite. I finished my drink, ready to begin my visiting. I daresay my life with Bobbie will be with me for the rest of my life.

On the concrete apron near the crossing a dog's foot had left a deep print before it had set. I'd seen that paw print for years. The dog is long dead.

(It was no way to say good-bye.)

My engineer is at the back of beyond. I thought I held her like a bird in my hand, happy to be there.

She is escaped from her cage. Little I knew: I'd never been caged. Who will catch her now?

This morning I woke at dawn. Bobbie had got up off her rug and was sitting at the window looking out at the silent eastern sky. When she felt me move and look at her she bent down and took a few licks from her water dish, turning her head to glance at me, then back to her deep gazing into the watery pinks of dawn where they drifted down the sky to the sharp, geometrical edges of human habitations, where night still was. It was a strange thing, not knowing her mind, or what horizons she saw.

Remember the time when *our* horizons were wider? When we thought our concern for water on this water planet would help spread a tablecloth for the whole world?

The Miser

Donna McDevitt is a miser; a woman of great debility, but basically too tough to know she's lonely. I suppose money is its own reward. She lives a few streets away in Liverpool Street; her house has a backyard and three storeys; it's made of stone that was cut and chipped by hand, the parallel marks of the masons' combs falling in one direction on one stone and at a different angle on another, like showers of rain in different winds. It stands on a larger block than other houses. She's noted for taking the bodies of other people's dead animals, boiling them and serving their meat to her own pets, which she loves and tends. When one of her dogs dies, it feeds the others.

There's a lot of protein going to waste, she says. She wishes she had the rights to the bodies of people. Her eyes gleam when she sees the clumsy, short-winded pigeons on the path outside.

Her face always looks strange and drunken, like an aged and derelict rock singer in pain. Twice she snorted with the effort of getting her breath as we talked and once, on the heels of a cough, farted. I was about to say: 'Who contributed?' but let it go.

I go to see her as often as I can: she's eighty-seven and doesn't get out like Georgina. Doctors had treated her at various times for head bounce, foot fester, labial pus, tongue crumble, lung quake, hand bunching, nipple destruction: she was a walking catalogue of decay. Last time I visited her I looked in her eyes and saw a street perspective receding from me, each house frontage diminishing to a narrow rectangular sliver of masonry in the distance, and at the end blending unselfconsciously with a line of tombstones clearly discernible at the end of the road. I guess I was once in Lidcombe looking towards Rookwood cemetery.

On the way to Donna's Bobbie had a slide down the slippery dip in a tiny park, legs stiffly out in front and sliding on her bottom. She has a way of putting her ears back and slitting her eyes that's so like a smile.

I was reasonably steady on my feet when I reached her house, made my presence known and got her to take her pets to another part of the house. When I looked in her eyes this time I saw a valley and the sort of bush you see out past Wiseman's Ferry. Looking closer, I saw a settlement of people living off the land, and some of them, at the water's edge, were washing their clothes in the river, just as they do in parts of France to this day, rubbing them on stones and dipping them back in the water.

'You're looking well, Donna,' I supplied. I told myself she was lonely because she was alone. This made my visiting worthwhile. But was she lonely? Once I tried to show her a photo of a sick little girl having a ride on Bobbie's back in the park, but she waved it away, not interested in little girls, only in Donna McDevitt.

'My father's father owned one hundred and twenty houses,' she said. 'My father owned one: the house he lived in. I've got them nearly all back. Not the same ones, but a hundred and eighteen. Two to go.'

She told me the same story each time.

'He lost them in a card game, a regular card game with his friends. Christmas Eve and every one of them pissed as newts. The stakes went up, the winnings went up, losses went up. He lost one house after another until there were five left and lost the last five on the turn of a card. The game was played in true sporting spirit and one hundred and twenty houses were redistributed among his friends. They had no houses before. Now he had just the one he lived in. His friends were happy. Friends! Sporting spirit! Games!' And she cackled, but the edge of disappointment was there, over the two she hadn't made up. Perhaps she never would, now, but those two houses, and the others she'd got back, were holding her together, and doing it well. I've never understood the puzzle of personal property; how, for some, losing property is losing part of one's self. All I know is losing people that are part of one's self.

'How about some coffee?' I said, just to remind her she was hostess. But there were no flies on *her*.

'I'm so sorry!' she said. 'I've just run out of coffee! What a shame! Oh dear!' And she wrung her hands, spotted with age. She'd always run out of coffee. I don't think she noticed when I walked out. I left her house and walked past the corner shop towards the new infants' school.

Out of one house, as if out of the throat of a trumpet, came Chopin's 'Raindrop Prelude' driven by massed brass bands farting, blurting, thumping, crashing. That's the sort of day it was going to be.

The photograph I'd tried to show Donna had been taken near the swings off Art Gallery Road. The child had cancer and knew she was dying. She was nine and frail and her skin dead white with blue veins, and Bobbie was so gentle. At the end they were changing her blood every few days until it seemed cruel to draw out a death so long.

They told me when she went, at one in the morning. As the phone rang I'd been looking out of my window at the green light they bathe Captain Cook in as he stands there in all weathers holding his right arm up for no good reason. *She* would never discover new lands, or anything now, and have no statue. I've even forgotten her name.

On the corner I was overtaken by the Penfold's dray, all painted up with curlicues and nostalgia, and the big-footed mare splashed one front hoof down in a puddle and wet my shanks as I stood there. I was right: it *was* one of those days.

When the Bobbie you love is much younger than you are, you feel often helpless to keep her out of all dangers, yet you know you can't be bending over her all the time with outstretched wings.

I remember the time I got the curved fishbone out of her throat before the doctor came. I still go cold when I think of it.

Heaven may grow full of holes and leaky, and the world crumble, but I refuse to run away from my love, or surrender to failure. My hopes will never drown, or drift away like smoke. My own refusal to let go, or let myself go, is the deepest prayer I am capable of.

My engineer believes the dreams of monsters bring forth humans. How could her soul become hard and without passion? Only death could cause that. Some things she says are so annoying! Yet not so annoying that I get annoyed.

In the Domain, just above the underground entrance to the parking station, Bobbie played with a wagtail. The pert little thing took off vertically, darted and flew so quickly and cleverly, landed and swivelled its body and tail, and Bobbie was delighted. There are such marvellous things to see and be part of on this crusted, puddled, iron ball of ours!

As we walked home I asked her: 'Shall we go and see Willie Wagtail tomorrow?'

She looked up at me with eyes I expected to be full of affection and trust, but weren't.

Perhaps she resents me talking to her as if she is a child. I bet she knows I'm still smarting from long-ago failures that can't ever be communicated.

Some of them I can't even explain to myself.

Even Sleep I Resent

Today we walk past the new infants' school. The future is here. Criminals and police of the future are here, too. What must we do with them, Bobbie, so the future will not condemn us and curse our behaviour and consider it would have been better if we'd not been born?

There isn't a child in sight, but a sort of hum comes from the classrooms. Bright pictures and cut-outs are stuck on the windows, facing in. When I see children, specially a lot of children, I feel like a monster from space: all face and no body, or a face with things attached to me, hanging down like helpless tendrils. While they gallop around like happy animals.

I hope their teachers are preparing them for life. And remembering that preparation for life *is* a part of life, that learning requires the learner to be interested and excited. Ah, all the things I could tell the young now!

⊂⊃

Someone had sprayed up on a brick wall:

THE FUTURE IS HERE.
IT WORKS: WE DON'T.

Perhaps the children singing inside the building saw it every day and naturally took no notice of it. I hoped so: songs I often sing I seldom mean.

As I walked on with Bobbie I grumbled to her, 'What sort of world are we preparing them for, darling? Where the cottage industries carried on in backyards are lamb dyeing, dog painting, bird decoration, cat colouring, horse beautification and disguise; where grants are solemnly given to young people to teach dogs to bark, to instruct cats to play with wool, to impart birdsong to birds?'

In the gutter was a piece of flex, such as they fit to electric irons. I wonder what its history was. Had it been used to terminate some loved one? To hurt a child? Or someone who welcomed the surprise and surge of warmth that pain brings?

Perhaps I was falling victim to one of my besetting sins, and growing afraid too easily of perfectly ordinary things, imaginary or not.

(When she was small, she was so like me. Her tiny hands, with their patterns of lines and creases — just like mine. And both little fingers bent at the tips.)

My engineer is strong; she says no person is made for one person only. Her strength is killing me. But I will not lie down and die. Even sleep I resent, which forces me to forget, briefly.

Last night the breeze was from the north and the scent of flowers and pollen and new growth was riding soft on the air. Ever since I was seventeen the smell of spring has lifted me up and put new strength into me, so that nothing seems impossible. I *will* be cheerful.

Two years ago when I was bitterly sad I planted a peach stone in the largest of the earthenware pots on the roof — I think it was two years ago. Perhaps 'planted' is too gentle a word. I meant to push the seed into the earth as an intrusion, as something I wanted to do whether anyone else wanted it or not, an aggressive action, a punishment for my misery.

It surprised me by sprouting. It's now a bit short of two metres high. Perhaps it was three years ago. There are even knobby bud-like lumps on its branches. I wonder if a tree planted in a pot could ever amount to anything.

The older I get the more I seem to be tormented by green spring and new growth. They're always new to me, yet never strangers.

There Has To Be a Lover and a Loved

The Conqueror's Arms was two bar-girls short, and snapped up two well-spoken girls who presented themselves in answer to Ivy's ad.

'It's a pleasure to have educated girls around,' boomed Ivy, sipping her vodka.

Outside in Cathedral Street, a priest passed by, counting out her prayers like something you hold in your hand. It was the day the corpse was found in the Domain, sitting on the seat on the eastern side of the ventilation outlet to the parking station. Covered in cockroaches.

'You ever have conversations with them?' I angled. I don't enjoy being sarcastic usually, but Ivy was a sucker for an educated voice, and anyway.

'Oh, yes.' Then, 'In the breaks, of course.' Time was money.

Why did I have a fit of uncontrolled laughter just then? It had to do with the cost of time. No one else laughed. It went on for some time, but I'm so used to being overtaken by sudden funnies like this that I wasn't in the least embarrassed.

They presented as Amy and Nora Triptyline. Ivy didn't query the surname — these were troubled times. They were of the old breed of graduates: Arts tickets and nowhere to use them. Here they were, serving slops over a bar to women who largely didn't know what anthropology was, but their present studies were confined to the cultural and physical environment of the tavern bar.

Amy was blonde and Nora brown. Nora wore a deep tan even in winter; she was the prettier. She was so proud of her tan that she displayed a massive quadrilateral of brown back always. No definition, no muscles: only this huge smooth surface. It worried at me; I found myself thinking of it at odd times.

Amy was the fierce one; her face, from the side, was vertical from forehead to chin, with small recesses and bumps for eyes, nose and lips. She carried her head forward like one of those bullying sea-gulls in the park that point their heads at others and run at them, making them run away, or even, as a last resort, take to the air. That sort are old, with dark red legs like dried blood, and retired. The park is their retirement village; they are pensioners on public scraps, just like any other pensioners.

I saw Amy and Nora off duty in Chez Ivy's several times.

'These'll never be on the game,' Ivy bantered. 'They'll never get the price.' And expected me to laugh. But their world was each other.

'Each of them is convinced the other loves her passionately,' I corrected.

'It's just a touch of Bilitis,' said Ivy.

They always kept close together, and moved into a new room attached to the back of a house in Cathedral Street. One of the girls who lived there, Victoria, who had a part-time job at the tractor warehouse feeding the dogs that guarded the automatic surveil-lance and stock-counting machines, had had her eye on a white timber packing-case that housed a machine sent over from tractor headquarters. (The rest of the world was headquarters: Australia was still an outpost, after all the years, all the words; it would be a long time before it was anything more than that.)

When the complete product was sent from overseas, the tractor was assembled and trucked away and the packing-case was scrap. Victoria offered to take it off the yard manager's hands. Five dollars later she put it on one of the warehouse trucks and it was landed holus bolus at the house in Cathedral Street. She took a few days off (the yard manager only expected her when he sighted her: he had to try to get near the dogs to feed them and it wasn't easy — they were trained to be savage) and she fitted some corrugated-iron windows, cut out a door and swung it on hinges she got from an old shed that had lost its door. The new room went in under the back of the house where the piles were tall, supporting an informal extension to the upper floor. There was headroom for a short person if she was prepared to bend a bit.

The girls seemed pleased with their packaging-case room; as with the rest of the house, there wasn't much rent to pay. They just had to buy for themselves, and chip in to the kitty if someone else in the house was doing it tough or otherwise fatigued.

I always said hullo to them, but they didn't take to me. Others said hullo, but the two girls didn't take to them either. They said about as much to strangers as did old Ben Boulevard, the white cockatoo in the lobby at the Boulevard Hotel in better days. They were good barmaids — not much beer went in the slop tray — but they refused to take their breaks separately. If the tavern was busy in their break, the manager or Ivy had to pitch in and help the other girl. Amy and Nora kept together all the time and didn't talk to anyone else.

But they talked to each other. Holy shit! How they talked. They argued a lot, commented a lot, pleaded a lot, complained a lot, shouted a lot, cooed a lot, whispered a lot. Both thrusting and assertive, their voices piercing. And they tell me those voices continued far into the night, down in Cathedral Street.

They were too much alike.

There has to be a lover and a loved, even if the roles change from time to time, or every few minutes. But both trying for the aggressive part at the same time and the submissive part at the same time: that was the brick wall. It was as if they read the other's mind, and one, seeing the other was going to be submissive and soft, had to be submissive and soft too. It was a competition.

When they got sick Ivy insisted, 'Give 'em a gargle with amniotic fluid!'

One jesting Jessie in the bar actually ordered from the beer company a thirty-five-tonne tanker of amniotic fluid, giving the address of Chez Ivy. It took weeks to sort out that shemozzle.

Ivy visited them in case they were in need, and ordered, 'Get in lots of milk! Keep 'em in bed and take 'em back to babyhood! That's the ticket! Babies drink lots of milk.' Amy was thirty, Nora thirty-one. Ivy said atrocious things to make them fight back.

'When they start going me scone-hot, they're on the mend.'

We are all primitive, I guess; wanting, at bottom, to own others. And that in us that isn't primitive is changeable, disappearing, negligible, misty, a trick of fashion.

Amy and Nora got better, but some of the rougher women christened them Over and Under, and they couldn't take it. Next thing they'd left Chez Ivy and Cathedral Street.

⌒

There they are today, splashing about in our old school swimming pool. Bobbie and I approach from Forbes Street, and they are still talking, still competing. We get up close to them and Bobbie puts her nose down gingerly to smell the water. I ask them how's things, but all they can talk about is this Professor Stonefish who has a marvellous group therapy session.

As we walk away, they go back to arguing. 'I'm what I am! Not some offshoot of what you want me to be! You can't have what you want — that's not life! That's only on paper.'

'I wish I'd heard the first part of *that* conversation,' I confided to Bobbie.

They must have heard my voice, for their voices stopped. Only for a second.

'What arrogance! She doesn't love that thing! She's just showing off. We'd see it if she *did* love the bloodthirsty thing! We could tell!'

Bobbie — a thing! I turned to look at her, bent down and took her beautiful face in my hands.

'I do love you. You know I do. I'm not just a gay deceiver.'

My mother, laughing with her eyes, said the same words to me, just as I'd said them to my first Bobbie. But my mother went away forever the week after she'd said them to me, and Bobbie was the one who went away from me. There was no pattern, apart from the words. My mother did what she wanted to, and so did Bobbie; and that's courage, I know it is. But pain for me; pain that stays.

> *My engineer fears*
> *one of the hardest things*
> *is to learn from the mistakes*
> *of mothers.*

The construction works in Bourke Street has its excavation surrounded by high, white-painted sheets of board, with a few holes for passers-by to look through. The women on the pneumatic equipment are at least twenty metres down, working on the sandstone walls they have penetrated, material no humans had seen before they saw it. Bobbie stood up on her hind legs and took a quick peep through the square hole.

'When the past does bob up, they piss it off,' I assured her. 'The past is different from what they think. It's not buried, it's all round us. We're all archaeologists, if only we can see.'

Bobbie looked at me, saying nothing. I wish she had some sort of expression in her sleek eyes.

She understands me very well, I think. I wish *I* did. I really must try to stop drinking so much. If we are learning animals, why can't I learn?

As we walk on, two deadbeats are sitting on the footpath near the gutter step talking to each other, and they ask me the time. I don't understand why derelict persons always need to know the time.

All the Senseless Luxury of the West

Linda Batt had been a work-habituation team leader, and the day she dropped dead in Martin Place — just by the earthenware blind girl with the disadvantaged legs, box chest and blue stick who stood near the Pitt Street flower-seller — she was coming back from buying a lottery ticket in Barrack Street. She was buried two days later and because she had requested it they interred her in her best business suit — the two-piece with the silk blouse and blue tie to match her eyes, and her best shoes; the outfit she wore on the day of her death. She was fifty-one, an uncomplaining sufferer from toe-drop. Much missed by the girls of the work-habituation unit and the regulars at Chez Ivy. She looked really lovely at her viewing, the pale satin casket-lining setting off her suit, and her complexion quite pink. Gone to nothingness and God.

A week later the lottery was drawn and the Hopeless Five syndicate was sixty thousand dollars better off. Every one of the hopeless four had the same thought. It had been Linda's turn to get the ticket, so where was it? They went to the lottery office, but no luck. You had to produce the ticket. It wasn't made out in her name but in all five, so if they had the ticket they were sweet, sweet as a nut.

Freda Livingston had the idea first, but didn't mention it. Josie Small thought the same thought. Billie Melville and Evie Schonk thought of it together next day when they were first at the bar. Evie paid for the beers and, with the change in her hand, turned to Billie, whose face had lit up with a keen, sharp look.

'I've got an idea,' Billie said.

'So have I,' Evie said.

'Is it what I'm thinking?'

'In her suit?'

'In her best suit, for sure.'

'Has to be. They looked all through the house.'

'No risk. That's it.'

They waited for the other two and their faces told the story when they came in through the brown glass front door of the Lover's Arms. There was a little pause for explaining to Billie that their shares were still one-fifth each, since the deceased estate got the share that should have been Linda's. Even then Billie thought it didn't seem fair, Linda being dead, having neither existence nor use for money.

They went to their solicitor, the solicitor went through channels, Linda was dug up and in front of official witnesses and the participants in the prize, the ticket was found in her breast pocket.

'Good old Linda,' they said in the pub that afternoon. They were giving the Chez Ivy a rest to avoid all the snips.

'She didn't look too bad, did she?'

'I thought she'd look much worse than that for the time she's been there and the warm weather.'

(Linda was one of those who'd been to see me; she asked about toe drop and anal languishment. She was cured now.)

'Must be cool down there.'

'No change of air, but.'

'Don't any of the rest of you go dying on us with tickets in your pockets, will you?'

'Anyone feeling sick?'

No one was feeling at all unwell.

'What if it hadn't been there?' asked Billie.

'Then we'd find the employee of the burial people who did the laying out,' said Freda.

From the pub windows they could see the rain spearing down into the street and bouncing up in fierce splashes. On the roof of a small block of flats down Crown Street a woman was standing out in the rain hanging her washing on clothes-lines suspended between two vertical timber posts. There were fourteen nappies.

'Look at that poor bitch,' said Josie. 'While we haven't got a care in the world.'

Evie said pityingly, 'Pegging out her washing in the rain, while we sit here, surrounded by all the senseless luxury of the West.'

They spluttered into their beer, and looked round at the bar with very fat and satisfied looks on their faces. They went on to talk about how the other half lives, and how to go about finding out. Up to now they'd been in the worse half. I'd thought of them as a unit that would be somehow lame or lopsided without one of their number, but one was gone and the survivors were on an even keel and laughing.

The engineer said we are enjoined to love everyone, but no one in particular. Saying this to me is like giving back its wine to a vine.

I'd last seen Josie, Billie, Freda and Evie together at the wine and food day of the Hyde Park Festival. It was one of those eating and drinking promotions — the Festival of Guts, I call it. Bobbie and I walked through the crowds in the morning when people were

queueing and standing, and again around five when most were
sprawled on the grass. For days the park was littered with broken
chips of plastic cups. Those four were lying in the sun near Captain
Cook, not far from three of the Australian wine promotion stalls.
They were drunk.

I hate crowds. A tavern full of people I like, if it's in Cathedral
Street, but I prefer small groups. If I ever get caught in the middle
of a large mess of people I begin to tremble; my hands, my arms,
my body, my legs, I tremble all over. I'm so afraid.

After the Festival, council women put hoses on the ground in
the northern section of Hyde Park. Days later I could still smell
the feet of barefoot crowds on the nude earth. The smell was like
the hot socks of schoolkids who'd worn them all day. Still, grass
would come again and smell sweet. Grass seeds were spread for
this reason; they were keeping all the pigeons busy and on their
feet. Hungry seagulls walked near them, puzzled that others could
bear to eat such dry tack.

The Sin against the Bicuspid Incisor

I've always considered, Bobbie, that my life was spoiled at six years
of age. It was then I knew — I grasped the idea — that mother wasn't
mine, alone. I don't mean other kids, though that would probably
have turned my tiny mind: I mean she belonged to so many groups,
so many other people. All pressure groups. There was the Anti-gun
League, the Australian Premonitions Bureau, The Dog Society,
Management Associates, Anti-Vivisection, penal reform, Australian
Intuitive Force, the small farmers' lobby, the High Income Group,
University Lecturers' Union, Landscape Engineers' Society, and so
on. They say where two or three are gathered together, that's the
beginnings of group therapy. Like so many people in those days
she was attracted to astrology, personal development courses and

pop psychology, and at that time those ideas were only a step away from becoming pressure groups. They knew as little then as we do now who they were or what they were; you and I know, Bobbie, that this is a matter of discovery, and it's part of, and happens a little, if we're lucky, every day.

Perhaps when I say my life was spoiled I mean she could no longer give me undivided attention twenty-four hours a day. Now I think of it I'm ashamed I ever thought such a thing. But why be ashamed of being a child? A little selfishness at six isn't unusual. As a matter of fact it probably amounts to something like the sin against the Bicuspid Incisor, doesn't it? That's how serious it is.

Now, Bobbie, let's not eat those cats. Eight cats were in a small driveway, four on the concrete, two on a brick wall, and two on the roof of a red car as we passed. Not for long. The sight of Bobbie seemed to suck them under the car. Further down the street we passed the front door of a new advertising agency. Bobbie was nice about the cats, she didn't even look back to add to their fright.

Come on, Bobbie! Let's step it out to the pub! If I don't get a drink soon I'm just in the mood to pick a fight with God!

The engineer never knew her father, but who ever did? His part in my life was out of place, like a laugh in the middle of a fight.

Visitors see dull and grimy streets here: I see lovely dull and beautiful grimy. The soul of this city is the sun — with its light the meanest streets skip and play like happy children.

Two very fat kids were playing hopscotch on the bitumen foot-path, with a watching toddler nearby in a pusher. We walked off the footpath on to the road to get round them. The two playing hoppy watched Bobbie without moving, but the smallest one put out both arms as if Bobbie was merely a walking version of a toy she might cuddle.

At the corner we looked back. The fat kids were still there, taking the stairs to heaven by way of hopscotch squares numbered 1 to 8. I took the ones to Cathedral Street and the Lover's Arms.

Why do I drink? I suppose it's because it's not abstract, like other ways to oblivion; it's more direct, there's more to do; it's more social, more cheerful. The sadness of losing someone lifts for a few hours.

Nothing Can Keep Males Out

In my city, everywhere I walk I've been before: the ground knows me. Ella Baroni detests the city, and hides from it down in a cave near water level in Woolloomooloo Bay, out of sight of Art Gallery Road. Before coming to the City of Women Ella had been in industry, one of those converted who had internalised the goals and methods of a large organisation. Her surrender of herself had been voluntary and complete.

'I considered that, in general, the goals of the organisation were superior to mine,' she told me. Something I could never have said about any organisation.

This was a thick, formidable woman, with heavy features and a pinkish colour suffusing her brown face. You've seen, Bobbie, how often derelicts have a deep tan unattained by the most dedicated sunbather. Her eyelid displacement was minimal.

When I'd climbed down and walked the few metres over broken rock to her cave with Bobbie, Ella was sitting in the entrance on a rock spread with something woollen, lifting a glass of colourless liquid to her puffy lips.

'Have a drink,' she offered immediately. Nothing mean about Ella. It was methylated spirit; there was a film of fingerprints and greasy marks around the glass. (She had been convicted, in industry, of using conflicting voice commands to a computer with intent.)

'Got a cold one?' I asked cheerily. I think. Over near her pile of possessions was a small brown bottle, narrow-necked and with hunched shoulders; it was a very old bottle, probably valuable — more valuable, perhaps, than the two of us put together. A large piece of pie-crust nestled against it. Pie crust?

'Sure there's a cold one.' She rose with an agility not all fifty-four-year-old women possess whose hearts have been broken by industry and detection in fraudulent conversion. Over by the water's edge she pulled up a stout string with a bottle attached.

'It was only a joke,' I said a trifle weakly. Methylated? Me? there was no trace on the limbs she exposed during her movements of the tendon corrugation and shoulder shrink she once complained of.

I sipped it. I made sure the sip was only a drop.

'No tax on this lot, eh?' she said heartily, swigging hers. And looked out across the water towards the ships of war tied up motionless by Garden Island. 'Tax, girl, tax. The ransom you pay to protect you from the wrath of the penniless.'

'We need no protection, Ella.'

'We *are* the wrathful penniless, aren't we?' she agreed. 'Yet we still pay tax. It's a ransom we pay to the rich to support their property, their markets, their roads, their explorations, their luxury, their industries, their safety. We buy their goods and foot the bill for all their subsidies. The Department of Defence has one purpose: to defend the rich. It's their country.'

'Could be,' I said doubtfully. Every sensible person knows who governs, and it isn't the poor. Laws apply to the poor. But why argue with what is? I didn't want any confrontations with Ella, physical or verbal.

Once, a year or two ago, returning from a walk past the place where a Queen had stepped ashore, I came upon Ella beating an iron bar against a driftwood box, breaking it up, but also, she said, having practice. At what? She didn't answer, but I heard later that she had put that bar across the neck of a young homeless woman who had climbed down the rocks and wandered near her cave. The girl was found dead, later, from exposure, and Ella had gone missing a few months.

'Never mind "could be",' she said warningly. 'Thought power' — she tapped her forehead — 'faster than light. This brainbox can think from one end of the universe to the other in less than a second. Faster than light by a factor called the universe.'

'Do you get many visitors?' I asked, thinking of the dead girl.

'Just a watchdog.'

'A dog?' I saw no dog.

'A male.'

'What breed?'

'Human.'

'What do you mean "watchdog"?'

'A man. He keeps busybodies away with his hypodermic. Lives in the next cave.'

'He's one of the people that cut women!' I said, alarmed. 'Do you realise you're harbouring a male?'

'You can't keep them out, Doc. Nothing can keep males out. He's handy for me; I don't bother him and he don't bother me. Never harms me. If you ask me, those others bring it on themselves.'

'You're not right in the head! You'll get expelled from the City for harbouring!' I was thinking only of her safety and preserving what little comfort she had.

'Ah well, Doc. We have to make a few compromises. If I get caught I'll tell them I keep my mind in this paper-bag.' She picked up a brown paper-bag from under an old alarm clock, blew it up — the bag — and twisted the end to keep it full of air. 'They'll believe old Ella.'

'I suppose so,' I said. But thinking of her dangerous behaviour, and her calm recital of it made me feel I was a small Australian animal, exposed to attack and a long way from my burrow. Also, I was losing fur.

'You wouldn't turn me in, Doc, would you?' And smiled at me, as if I was a subordinate.

'Certainly not!' I replied indignantly, as much at her expression as the principle of the thing.

She smiled comfortably at me again and finished her warm spirit. I took matters into my own hands, never mind manners, and poured the rest of mine into her glass. She understood.

'Keeping your holy guts for good Scotch, Doc?'

The engineer declared I have neither malice nor forethought, but my breath is strange when in fear of the future.

At night in Hyde Park the possums come down on the grass and have a look for tasty scraps, even getting into the bins.

The Botanic Gardens, though, are alive with movement during the dark hours; small animals forage among the plants, and some climb trees; some night predators stay and hunt, others set out on a night flight south and a little east, to the many hectares of Centennial Park. These last fliers number hundreds, and fly swoopingly, jerkily, with sudden changes of direction and elevation, and sometimes you can hear little squeaks from them. They come over past my building — three, five, one at a time — and if I put my head out of the window and make little squeaks at the top end of my voice, they sheer off and sometimes turn right away.

At night the air quivers invisibly, making lights dance about on the northern shore; the dark grips me; I am grateful.

Even the Derisive Derelicts Are Asleep

At times we could not predict, our whole City was troubled with the sound of knocking at night. When it happened first, women complained their front doors banged like drums after midnight, yet when they went to answer the knocking, the sound seemed to come from houses round about. Was someone locked out? Was there a ghost in the streets?

Some of the armed women shot off rifles at the sound, particularly when they were drunk. Sometimes the knocking would cease, when rain came, then resume when the weather was clear. It was never constant, we had no chance to get used to it. It would begin late, stop, start in the early hours, fade away, begin again before dawn. Then stop for a week.

When they resumed hostilities, they would beam amplified sound all over our City; often it took the form of desperately heavy breathing with an insistent heartbeat, fading, then coming up like an emergency of the heart, alarmingly.

It was no use complaining to our own police or public servants: they were just as much outside our day-to-day society as their counterparts were in any possible enemy territory. Anywhere you walked on those nights the sound had the same loudness; there was no place nearer to it, or further away.

When they tired of this form of torture, they sickened us for days on end with the smell of roasting pork. It was bearable the first few times, but now no one roasts pork in the City of Women. The enemy live still in their ferocious past; they are at home in the world of aggression, the atmosphere of the shark where death and war are not dirty words. I wonder, were butterflies pierced and mounted before the technology of the pin?

☞

Our doctrine, Bobbie, is that many things and many people are in each one of us. Some of these are small and will never develop, others will show promise and fill us like sails; we will encounter winds from places we never dreamed of. In us are gods we didn't believe in; the past, the future, time; a richness we have allowed to develop because we locked ourselves away from their sterile world, their blunt, piglike minds, their instinctive hatred and exclusion of freedom in its many forms.

Bobbie, we say: Free yourself, for a free person has the most value for the community of those she loves. We say: Free yourselves from all things, if you like! Not to destroy or ignore them, but to stand at a distance and really *see* things in a second perspective.

We are different from our enemy: we have no need to impress ourselves on objects; we have different attitudes to property and to owning things; we don't need the sort of life they would inflict on us. We are one family and many families.

～

It is late at night. Across the harbour the far suburbs are slabs of darkness pricked with street-lights and tiny lit windows. Here in the City — which is my home because it is alive in me — the escalators have all stopped, and most building lights dimmed. Lights are still on in the Law building; two high blocks have coronets of light; Centrepoint is lit from below; the Hyatt sign is on; the Gazebo crown is white; the Art Gallery roof is all light. Black at the top of William Street is the Coca Cola sign. It is the end of the day out there past our City limits for the bewildered, arrogant young, the hordes of late TV watchers, secretive freaks and fetishists, insomniac homosexuals, dirty-minded wives, lecherous politicians, masturbating husbands, anguished intellectuals. Even the derisive derelicts are asleep.

Now and then a car races up William Street. A heavy truck comes up from Woolloomooloo Bay, its load heaped in two white piles visible over its high sides; it stops for the lights and turns up Boomerang Street past the brown cathedral — black now — and hauls itself away into silence. I notice now the two cranes at Number 11 wharf are moving across from one of the 'Lake' ships — is it the *Lake Eildon?* the *Barrine?* the *Lake Eyre?* the *Hume?* — to a waiting truck. The floodlights are violet and piercingly bright.

They are not attacking us tonight, and I am confident that this is one time I won't worry myself sick. I wish my worry would gather itself into little puddles, then run away, like my anger does. It leaves a mess for a while, but soon disappears.

My mind feels mobile, furtive as a fox: I hope I sleep. Sooner the bumpy ground of dreams than lying, with sharp ears, waiting for my mind to turn off and my thoughts to let go of me.

The engineer subjected me to due process of fear. When I

protested, she looked at me as if by accident a dog had barked a word.

In bed tonight my heart seemed to be making a lot of effort for no big reason; big heartbeats shook my whole diaphragm and stomach area. They speeded up a bit when I became aware of them, and if I took a deep breath and let it out, they slowed as I breathed out. Every few months I notice this sort of thing happening — I daresay it means nothing. I went to sleep hoping I wasn't going to have one of those dreadful nights — when you dream you've never been born.

Sometimes I think it would be better to be an artesian waterdrop for thirty thousand years under New South Wales than a woman — short-lived, and salt tears most of the time.

I built my life up, strong and high; now it is falling. Time tells me I must gradually let go, but I do not believe I must. I will let go suddenly, and not till then.

Ronnie

They called her 'the Judge': she was always saying, 'Cop this!' *This* was usually a back-hander somewhere about the body, though you could tell if she was really annoyed, for then the first blow was always to the face.

When Ronnie wasn't going off she was a nice guy. She tipped the scales at a hundred kilos — not all muscle, but near enough. She was immensely strong. She came in to the pub Saturdays. She was no Chloe, that's for sure, but who knows what the Queen of Sheba looked like?

On the way north to the races at Newcastle last month, with three of her mates from their home pub in Darlinghurst Road, she kept stopping to pick up male hitch-hikers until she found one with upper and lower dentures (don't ask me how they tested for this, but such males with their limbs held and teeth out, had no weapons at all) then kept driving while the others worked their will on the male on the back seat all the way to Cockle Creek.

'Come on, have one,' the other girls urged, generous with what they got for nothing. 'Have a lash.'

'No, I'll drive,' she said calmly. She loved driving. Used all the road, but she was good.

On the banks of Cockle Creek, teamed up with another fourteen girls of the travelling kind — eighteen in all — they worked on the male till he was in a bad way.

Ronnie pointed out that he was beginning to show signs of wear.

'Look, you guys, there's blood coming from the mouth of it as well as all down the length. And you've just about bitten its balls to bits. I say call it quits. This one didn't look any too bright on it to start with, either.'

His name was Vernon: it was tattooed on his thin little forearm. His pubic hair had been chewed and bitten out in clumps; it was now only a few straggles of vegetation at the outer edges. Fingers with sharp nails had lacerated his prostate — in the cause of helping it up time after time — until blood seeped from that place. He was in agony.

After another hour he seemed to slide quietly into a sort of sleep.

'I think it's in a coma,' says Ronnie. 'Give it your T-shirt, Bugs.'

Bugs was short for buggarise, though we shouldn't mention the instrument. Everyone has her thing; from one point of view there are no unusual desires.

They pulled a large T-shirt on to its body and remarked to the unconscious shape, 'Wait here, we'll be back later.'

'Here' was the side of the road. Vernon was really fucked and far from home.

'Someone'll be sure to pick him up before morning.' It was nice of them at last to use the personal pronoun about poor Vernon. And they went on their way north to enjoy the races. Later the whole seventeen of them found they'd copped a load.

⌒

Linda, the TV mechanic, played football with Ronnie.

'She and I played second-row. I don't get upset easily on the field. My job in the line-outs and tight play is to stop the opposition coming through. Many's the time I have hold of some girl's guernsey or neck or leg and she'll turn and take a smack at me. I never retaliate.

'Once, after a game, a guy that got two cautions — our kicker kicked both penalties — for socking me came over to me and said, "You're the first guy I ever played against that never hit back. I've played since I was ten and most of the girls would cut you to pieces and boil you down for soap without another thought." She was the tall, rangy type, hard as nails, the sort that when they get going never know when to stop.

' "Well," I said. "I'm there pulling you back and obstructing on the blind side of the ref, so I guess I must give you a bit of a stir. It's no wonder you do your block. It wouldn't be all that logical for me to stir you, get hit, then hit back because I was hit. Besides, those hits don't really mean much: I'm hot when they connect; I don't notice. And you're not usually on balance."

'She nodded her head, then shook it.

' "Then who was it clobbered me each time? It wasn't you. I had my eye on you, waiting for it. It was someone."

'It was someone, all right. Good old Ronnie. There was something in her make-up that couldn't bear to see a punch taken and no punch in return. Debit and credit, sort of; the germ of accountancy. She thought she was being a good mate.'

❧

When she went off her brain, it was different. Once when she was full and a stranger put her name up on the board for a game of pool, Ronnie took a dislike to her face.

'This is my pub,' she says, 'Beat it.' And rubbed the girl's name off the board. The girl looked round, saw plenty of curiosity but no sympathy, finished her half Scotch and made for the door and Cathedral Street.

Her actions were too slow for Ronnie and her pub loyalty. They amounted to what a cop, or an officer and a gentleman, would call dumb insolence. With her large white hands Ronnie got a full nelson on the stranger as she went past, and put her through the glass door, which opened inwards.

❧

She had a milk van for a time and each afternoon parked it in the pub lane, driving to and from it in her car. One Friday night as Ronnie was leaving, some driver honked her horn. Ronnie thought she was honking at her. Over she goes, hauls the woman from the car and whack! Petty Sessions Monday morning — four hundred dollars! Just for a jaw.

Next she sold plots for Invest in Rest, the new company flogging mini real estate. They also had a piece of the action in the furnace business, which was where the smart people were switching their money because of the high cost of plots.

While she was practising her sales spiel, she would read it over to me, getting it word perfect.

One thing she could never master, though, was the absence of the letter *n* in a phrase of their ad — 'Inurnment and Interment'.

Ronnie couldn't keep the extra *n* out of 'Interment.' 'Inurnment and Internment,' she'd say. I felt it was up to me to put her right, but she couldn't see the difference.

She sold a lot of business, anyway, because she went round in the daytime and the people at home were happy to have a cheerful woman at the door. She had a respectful voice and, when she tried, sounded extra sincere: the sort of sincere that drops its *g*'s and *h*'s and makes its sentences a bit clumsy, and hesitates over a word so the person at the door is right in there with the missing word, helping. She sounded like a real trier, and they lapped it up.

She laughed about it in the pub. Sometimes she'd have her week's quota done by Monday lunchtime, and her sales bonus by three the same day. The rest of the week was her own; there was golf, sailing, the races: she lived like royalty. And all because the public was anxious where their carcasses would be put when they dropped dead. The market was ripe for a self-destruct mechanism with no fall-out, she said.

⌒

One Saturday when she'd got a little drunk, but cheerful, a cop on her own in a car saw fit to stop her and tell her she was arrested.

'What for?' said Ronnie.

'You know.' But the cop wasn't game to try to get this one to blow in the bag, she might rip it or something. Besides, she was on her own, and it wasn't proper procedure. She tried to use the car radio but something was interfering with it.

'Get in,' she said.

'Why? What have I done?'

The officer thought a bit. There was sure to be a phone up the road. She got out her handcuffs.

'Here, hold out your hand.'

Ronnie thought for a moment or two and reluctantly put out a soft pink hand. There was something about so many convictions, wasn't there?

The cop put one handcuff on Ronnie, the other on the bumper bar of the car, and walked up the road.

When she'd phoned for help and walked back, the car was gone. Help came in the shape of a police car and two uniformed cops. She explained what she'd done.

'What did she look like?' the older officer said. She was the most senior sergeant in the district. The arresting officer described Ronnie.

'Get in.' And drove straight to the nearest pub, which happened to have a driveway leading to a backyard beer garden. There was the car, with Ronnie inside the double gate, still handcuffed to the car, but sitting on a seat at a beer table. Several empty glasses stood on the table. She still had money in her pockets and was smart enough to know that if the cop only had witnesses to her drinking now, she couldn't have any opinion about how much she'd drunk before. No legal opinion, that is.

The three officers got out and looked at her.

'Might have known it'd be you,' the sergeant said. 'Get the key.'

They unlocked her. No need to say anything. Everyone present, including the pub crowd, knew they had no case. The officers looked at each other, shook their heads.

The sergeant laughed suddenly. The other two laughed. Ronnie laughed, spluttering beer from a new pint everywhere. Some went on a sauce bottle on the table, ready for the barbecue later in the pub fireplace. She didn't mind.

'Have a drink,' she said.

They got in their cars and drove away. The young cop put it down to experience.

⌒

By contrast with Ronnie's calm competence in matters of violence, two women had a fight outside the Lover's Arms in Cathedral Street, a nasty, bitter fight: the hate was meant. I don't like to watch, but I couldn't help seeing some of it. I found myself thinking that they — men — do this sort of thing much better; when they use gloves and ritual, that is. Men can do it so coldly, or seem to; precisely and without hate. Somehow it's cleaner than this. I felt sick at their white faces and the spots of blood — and the expressions in their eyes. Particularly the eyes.

The engineer, source of love and wonder, said we were animals. She has a voice like the colour of roses made audible, and I have arms that are starving. We live in a world that I am proud to be an animal in.

Today the caretaker came to the door for something, and her Corgi, the Duke, scampered in. Before I could do anything to stop it, he'd gone right through to my bathroom and snatched a washer from the side of the bath. Poor thing, overweight and getting old, too close to the ground to do anything about any of the neighbouring females, he still enjoys the female smell he finds on a wet cloth. He slavered and chewed it. I pulled it from his mouth, it was torn and juicy with saliva. I threw it out.

When I enter the building, or meet the Duke on the footpath, he extracts his due of affection and notice, trotting over to me on his short legs for a pat, his thick body wiggling with the effort. He'll never recognise friends when he's on his way out for a walk: he won't take the risk that entanglements with people might delay the walk, perhaps even cancel it. But if you meet him just as he's about to go inside *after* a walk he'll welcome you like a long-lost friend and try to keep his freedom, such as it is, in the open air, and draw it out as long as the caretaker will allow.

I think of him as a little toll-keeper of attention and affection.

The sun was very bright today, the sort of day when the shadows themselves seem as bright as other days' sun.

The Dog with Bare Skin

Two of the kids I was at school with had military mothers — one a major, the other a sergeant. I don't know if Major Douglas knew

Sergeant West, but the sergeant was aware of the major's existence; probably the major was more aware of colonels and brigadiers and other majors.

The major resented the talk and dissent of intellectuals, journalists, teachers, all who would disarm the country and leave it a prey to some exotic political system.

The major bequeathed her rank to her daughter — she christened her Major Douglas.

Sergeant West, who in those days lived in an identical ranch-style house a few streets away, worked in the garden and with paintbrush to keep her house as trim as the major's. She was successful. The major was unaware of this rivalry, but it was spiritual sustenance to the sergeant.

'Major Douglas!' she stormed. 'How can that be a girl's name? What's she trying to do?' Since the sergeant had produced a child at nearly the same time, she decided to show scorn for the major's reverence for the Army, and assert the spirit of democracy: she called her daughter Sergeant West. The daughters grew up in the same suburb. Sergeant was the smarter, Major was captain of the basketball team; Sergeant ran quicker, Major had an even temperament that made her popular.

Now, Bobbie, after all these years, they've both found their way to the City of Women. They were both imbued with the competitive spirit in their youth, intent on licking the enemy, licking their opponents, licking their partners, wherever they found themselves. Both became community soil testers, vying with each other in the smallest detail; Sergeant to beat Major, Major to keep Sergeant at bay. And now they're old, like me — parents gone, all who know them gone: all they have in the world is their rivalry. Both want to be public savants, but in a city of talk they have no audience.

Envy! This invaluable imaginative device! How it makes for what used to be called progress. Now, instead of 'progress' they say 'movement', which can have direction like a river or water in a gutter, or it can be stationary as in boiling.

They're both here in Burton Street. Last time I saw Major she was being treated for the arm strangles; last time I saw Sergeant she was having leg wilt.

Here's the house, Bobbie. Listen to the two lonely crows overhead! On the tiny front space — you would have to smile while you said it was a verandah — sits Major with a tight mouth and her arm bandaged. I wave to her and Bobbie turns her head to look, but Major can only nod, and begins to look away at something else. There is a spotted paint cloth on the painted cement, along with two paint tins and a brush and a much-used tin for cleaning the brush. The paint on the brush is Spanish Gold.

Sergeant's house is closed; perhaps she is having treatment for her leg. A young woman has a dog on a lead; it stops at Sergeant's front gate — painted in Spanish Gold — to leave a blessing. It's a large dog, mostly German Shepherd, and has a bare patch as wide as your hand stretching over its back, a patch with no fur but looking like bare skin, almost shiny. The patch reaches over both sides and may even meet under the dog's chest, I can't see. Some sort of hormone deficiency, I guess, but it's not polite to volunteer suggestions to the young woman: dog owners take such things personally. We are past them, Bobbie and I, before the dog reacts, hurrying away with its tail down, which is natural enough, and its rear parts curved under, looking back in anxiety.

I wonder what it's like to be a large dog, used to most other animals you meet being smaller, and suddenly to pass a leopard in the street.

The engineer emphasised
there was a vast
deference between us
no puns could bridge.

Around the fountain in the park are beds of white roses. In July the Council ladies pruned them, and in a week, because of one of those false springs we often have in our winters, they'd grown new leaf. The new growth is well under way now and each time I pass them I talk to them, telling them to get a move on; I'm dying to be able to bend over and bury my nose in white petals. Small birds use space on the branches and forks as landing places, alighting between the thorns. There are even blue wrens back here in the park (they'd gone missing for years), foraging between blades of grass twice a day for their morning and evening meals.

I walk among a crowd of busy pigeons when suddenly they strike out with violent wings, frightening me, and beat the air to pieces at my feet. I can feel the fragments. Among the birds are some whose wings creak on take-off.

I feel like something heavy and lumbering among all this lightness of petals and birds, even if some birds do creak.

The House Where I Was Born

Here and there a ripple in the fabric of the suburbs speaks of a hill, a rise — once covered in trees and bush and grass, animals warily wandered there as they warily did all they did — now crowned with a house that was fine once, surrounded by the slyly aggressive millions of cheap houses; small, resentful. On weekends the traffic arteries used to swell with the domestic cars taken out so their drivers could feel and enjoy motion and being carried, the shopping places and the markets were packed with people gaping with incomprehension at people like themselves, and with understanding at the infrequent rich. (How is it people understand the rich with no effort, yet end their lives still not understanding or coming to terms with poverty, their poverty?)

Ah, Bobbie, we're full of philosophy today, aren't we? If philosophy is a heap of questions.

It's all part of my burden, my darling with the sleek head and penetrating eyes. All these emotions. I'm such a silly woman, you mustn't take notice of me. Such a load of emotion, it's been adding up, attaching itself to me and growing on me all my life. What shall I do with it? Where will I take them all? Do you unload emotions as Bunyan's Christian hoped to unload his burden?

It's so lonely without my real Bobbie.

‿

Where was I? (My new Bobbie walks alongside me, careful never to let me know how slow I am compared to her; she could gallop if she wanted.) Ah, the place where I was young. The I that was I then can't be seen there now. But it is there. It's there, Bobbie. Every presence continues, the world is rich with crowded presences. From this hill near Taylor Square we can see down the street to the harbour and the ships tethered in the stream, and from there across to the northern shore where I was a child. Let's stand a while.

⌒

I have the impression I am looking down from a height to the house where I was born. It's tiny, as things are when you come back to them after some years, tiny on a clay step; the step is set in the side of a low hill that's not steep but gently ascending. Is it far? Is it really a big house and I'm further away than I think? It's hard to see, difficult to know in such a way as to convince myself I am present at a moment tinged with reality. Or is the house so near it is only the size of a teapot?

I put out a hand and tip the house. It rocks on its foundations. (It's much larger than a teapot.) It tips over. The house is upside down; it's made of ceramic. There are holes underneath. What are the holes for?

Ah, there's an answer. From the holes come insects, they escape in the kindly air. No, they don't! They're not flying, even though they're above ground — they escape along a network of spider webs. I hadn't realised the similarity between birds' and spiders' movements so well before. The insects hurry along their lines to safety. Towards me. They knock against my net-webbed leg.

⌒

A gust of wind kept passing and returning, looking in to see my mind. Mother had died. My brother Lovelock said, 'Shall we have a funeral?'

'Of course we'll have a funeral.'

'Have you enough cash?'

'Yes.'

'We'll go halves then.'

Funerals are nice. I remember now. The last time I'd talked of money with Lovelock I'd been looking for a place where I knew a clay pit had been dug, a pit where the whitest clay was locked into the ground, though it came forth with persuasion and leverage. Mother wasn't dead then, not dead at all. Was this another mother in a previous existence? Was I dreaming mother's dreams of *her* mother? My head was full of half memories. They meant nothing to me like that — chopped off at the thighs. Besides, what brother? I had no brother: I'd given him up years before.

Suffering shit, Bobbie! My memories of childhood aren't clear.

It's as if everything happened to some other person. But Lovelock: he was useless. I got my first acquaintance with men from him, and I know from that that men can't possibly fit in here in the City of Women, with us. If you're nice, if you let them go first, if you wait for them to speak, if you say nice things, congratulate them, ask their opinion, then you are lower than they: you're weak. They can't form communities; they don't want with-ness, they want command; they won't ever live in peace.

It's not that I'm bitter. I mean I'm not bitter. After I'd got rid of Lovelock — out of my life, I mean — I marked time a bit. There was a frustrating thing with the postgirl, then later a family friend consoled me among her glasshouse vegetables. Before Bobbie filled my life.

I'm not bitter, Bobbie; men are something more than rejected women.

The difference — the central factor, if only I could penetrate that far — is in how the individual makes contact with the world. The secret is somewhere in there. Difference, division and enmity are bred there.

I think we'll walk over to the Domain. I'll sit and watch you jump up and pretend to catch the little grass butterflies, the white and pale green ones. Perhaps we'll see the people come and exercise their dogs: the thin girl with the Great Dane, the old lady with her white Alsatian. And if the little mongol girl comes, pulled in a billy cart by her two older sisters, we'll talk to them about school and they'll want to stop and pat your head, your neck, your back. The mongol in the cart will try to touch your paws and pick up your tail. And after we've all gone, we'll leave the park to the absorbed, inattentive trees thinking lofty thoughts, not ground ones; and to the sounds wrung from sorry bells. (They seemed so frightened, sometimes.)

Then I guess I'll walk along Cathedral Street a little way.

The engineer left me with permanent grief. She said my love is a prison for intractables. But I think less of the words than I do of the pink mouth they came from.

Sometimes I forget which Bobbie I'm talking to and which I'm writing to. The one that can read will have to sort out that problem. What does it matter? I'm talking to both, everything I have to say to the new Bobbie is addressed to the first one, the real Bobbie.

Now I'm at the end of this letter I look out the window. It's a clear night, full of distances. The thought of you rings in my head, and all the music you mean to me.

Remember those shells you gathered on the sea beach at Nambucca? I take them out sometimes and put them to my ear. I hear you in them, not the sea.

If only I didn't feel all this! If only I was a freckle on the bottom of Bathsheba as she waited for King David to come in to her — or a black, gleaming hair, hard by the tit of Helen of Troy.

If only.

But not dead, like they are. I know dying is only the music come to a stop, but I don't want it to be all over.

I dreamed you up from nowhere to come live in my heart; any time you like you're welcome to step back into your space there — it's exactly your shape.

The Raffle

The Workers' Arms hadn't been renamed after the men left.

Terry, who ran it, looked at girls the way girls look at expensive chocolates. She always had problems of over-seduction. It was the sort of pub where characters in slacks and shirtsleeves bowl up to you and lean over you and expect you to be in their raffle. How many tickets do you want this time? As if you usually made unreasonable demands.

You couldn't refuse to take at least one, even if you had a pet leopard on her haunches by your side, head intelligently up, eyes roving everywhere, blinking occasionally. It wasn't a matter of strength of character — at least I don't think so. I bought two to show my independence.

I was thirsty and Bobbie and I found a space at the bar and settled there. People are scared of her. Because she has such teeth she can, and will, kill and eat flesh. But she's not aggressive at all.

Round the dark side of the bar an elderly woman staggered to her feet from the low long bench on which she'd been sitting, her face trying to compose itself into a look of stability, firmness and concentration, her hands in front warding off collisions that could easily happen. Thank God I'm not an alcoholic, Bobbie. The rest of that poor soul's life lay plainly somewhere on a scale between miserable and horrible.

The counter lunch looked attractive from a distance. I got a plate and eating tools and sat with others at a small table. I was somewhat hungry, I'd skipped breakfast. A large young woman, Lonnie — who'd been one of *them* until she'd had her operations — had a little fun at my expense.

'Look out!' she said in alarm as I tucked in. 'Watch your fingers everyone! Look at those jaws! Mind the teeth!' Everyone looked at my activities, which their fuss in no wise diminished. She'd been a woman for five years, but still hadn't settled down.

'Going like a motor mower!' she marvelled.

I said nothing, but went on forking it in and swallowing. I had the curried sausages with peas, a few pieces of exhausted carrot and a dob of mashed potato with a distinctly cowed appearance.

'You made me miss three swallows,' she said reproachfully as the others laughed. Nothing could stop her old male habit of chaffing and leg-pulling and she wasn't aware of it.

'Shouldn't be eating swallows,' I said in a voice foggy with food.

I was just finishing, ready to wipe my plate with the rubbery white absorbent bread provided for wiping, when two of the shirt-sleeve gang bowled up and with a clumsy flourish handed me a baby wrapped in swaddling clothes. I dropped neither it nor my cool; simply cooed to the little thing, gave it a cuddle — it smelled surprisingly good — then put out my arms to return it. They'd gone. My companions watched my face.

'Now what?' said Lonnie.

'What do you mean now what?'

'You won it. You won the raffle. The baby's the prize.' And got up to go, but remembering I wasn't a regular, and sympathising, stayed.

'There's plenty'll take it if you don't want it,' she said kindly.

'I don't want it. I certainly don't want it.'

Bobbie put her head up. I lowered the baby so she could see it. Bobbie couldn't help herself, she extended her beautiful tongue and licked part of the little face. I passed the baby to big Lonnie, who took it away. She seemed to know what to do. Perhaps they'd raffle it again.

My lost engineer loved me once; she was glad of my love when she was young. I think of her now as a sea, open to all who swim or sail. I stand at the edge of its vast complexity, wanting to feel the surge of its powerful currents.

Dear Bobbie, now we have given up hoping that all, some day soon, will have enough to eat, may you never know how sad it is to eat alone. (We are the caring ones; but also the regular eaters; our sadness is social.)

Love and Marriage in the Lover's Arms

Old Joan and Gwen were drop-outs years before when that word meant something. Joan was sixty-eight; she'd been principal of a high school, and because of Gwen took an early retirement and left her job. They wanted to be together all the time. She also left her husband of thirty years. Suitably provided with cash, of course, which heals all wounds.

Love excuses all.

On one hand Joan had two fingers missing. Many years before, when she had been teaching in the hillbilly country of eastern Victoria in a small, remote community, she had caned a boy on the hand. The hand swelled, the swelling burst, became gangrenous, and two of the fingers had to come off. The boy's father, suspecting that the young principal wouldn't even cop a fine, turned up one day, chopped off two of Joan's fingers with boltcutters, and went home satisfied. He got three years. It wasn't a story Joan liked told.

Gwen had been single all her life, and by her own account had had only one lover. Only one! Who wasn't a real lover because he never got more than about the head of it inside her. She rationalised this into a fifty-year-old virginity, and Joan was well satisfied.

What did it matter, Bobbie? Who would have cared?

Joan was a small woman and carried herself like a little bird. With a voice like a lion. 'But I love ya!' she roared once and it rattled the glass windows that led to the space outside in the open air.

Love is the thing, Bobbie. One should try to love the whole world. Love is a bridge, a conveyance, a propulsion, not a chain fixing your position.

⟨⟩

Gwen was in love, too. She used a good dye for her hair and had such a good figure, legs and all, that young women in the street, overtaking her in their cars as she walked ahead of them on the footpath, would lean out and whistle, saying things to themselves like 'Aaaaaah!' When they passed and saw she was just an old boiler, they cruelly changed it to 'Ugh!' and 'Yech!'

'It's a miracle we're together after all these years,' Joan was reported as having said.

'We should have met at nineteen,' replied Gwen, ignoring their age difference.

'Fifteen,' loyally said Joan. Gwen didn't pursue it downwards.

'You know so much about love,' one said to the other.

'I can't think what you see in me,' said the other. I forget which said which, Bobbie.

'When the end comes, make it quick,' the gloomier one said. 'Tell me!'

And the protests, and explanations. And tender arguments.

I'd never actually heard them at it. I'd have been tempted to say to them: love isn't personal, you don't own it. You've only got a lend of it. It's only a chunk out of the universal love and you kid yourself it's yours. It is, but only to use. It doesn't belong to you. It can be taken away quickly, cruelly. I wonder what they'd have said to that, Bobbie love.

Around them, in the pub or in the park, were often couples that prattled lovingly while they hated each other's guts, or old couples that bickered constantly yet loved, together with any amount of combinations of appearance and reality; but they were blind and deaf to all about them.

They're here today; Gwen has her head bent, listening attentively to Joan's lingering kiss on her cheek. Gwen's feet are in sandals; she has wounded toes, the little one on each foot has its head raised in alarm.

They recounted their love to each other interminably, looked in each other's eyes, touched at every opportunity — hands, thighs, shoulders. Joan even liked Gwen to slip her shoes off and touch her with her bare feet, gnarled and veiny as they were. And the wounded toes. The thing that got me, though, was that they were continually writing. Joan wrote in notebooks, or sometimes, with no notebook on the table, caught up her notes when she went to the toilet, taking her bag. She had bits of paper constantly with her.

When I went over near them to use the red phone she would be writing down what Gwen had said, how she said it, how she looked, what crossed her mind. Everything that had a bearing on their love.

Yes, but don't forget, I wanted to say, a concern for detail, though it lights a quick fire, leads to the extinction of desire.

What right had I, though? They were old, and humanity, sympathy and love see further than telescopes. Besides, they had been spared the years of close cold knowledge; spared the lover stiff not with desire but boredom; spared the over-exposure; spared the bored lover leaking not the fluid of life but the acid of disillusion; spared the spent lover penetrating not the gate of love but the white-anted portals of some ghastly Luna Park; spared the loss.

Ah, my flock, my children, my guards, my drinkers, my troops, my little shoppers for the good of life, my litigants, my parasites, my patients, my prodigals, my beasts, my guerillas, my zoo, my dwarfs, my wives, my deformities — there is a tide in the affairs of women that comes on time and once a month, a march of memorials in blood down the calendars of your life, that taken at the flood will wash all men away.

What a pity it can't wash away bitterness, disappointment, emptiness.

⊇

They went everywhere together.

Gwen was strictly religious, and couldn't marry a divorced person, which Joan was, so when they were both killed crossing William Street up the hill from the pub one Thursday night (their bodies were run over by three cars before anyone stopped) the girls from the pub thought it was a shame they hadn't died married. It can't be all that common to be in love after fifty.

Ivy had a niece in high school who was handy with decorating and sculpture and so on; they got her to make two life-size figures of paper. You know, you wet and mould the paper to any shape, then when it dries out it keeps the shape and gets hard enough to withstand handling, and you paint it.

She made three figures of old Joan and Gwen; they put them in the lopped coral tree out in the beer garden at the back of the pub. When it started to rain they brought them in and sat them on two chairs in the barbecue, and got me to say the words that would marry them. Do you, Joan? And Do you, Gwen? And a chorus of the girls said 'I do' for them. By this time the real Joan and Gwen were providing three squares for generations — for a whole nation — of white worms. (Stop me when I talk like that, Bobbie, please!)

For weeks their hollow corpses sat there, married. Until a storm from the south-east flung water in great quantities over the wall and under the low roof, which did not meet.

They melted, relaxed and grew grotesque. The final mockery of a dried-out and disfigured permanence was spared them by the application to their feet two days later of a lighted match.

The blaze was brief. There's still a black mark on the underside of the roof to remind us of their bridal chair.

It was a great funeral.

Now when I touch the place with a finger, there's still some black carbon loose on the surface of the roof-metal; it comes off on my finger. Bobbie looks at me, wondering why I touched it. Or does she know? Seeing my own hand, I think of your two dear hands, and the many times they lay, beautiful, on your bed as you slept.

I think of your hands.

Why is it wrong — is it wrong? — to want my child, whose flesh came out of my flesh, where I can see her all my life?

Where William Street curves off into Boomerang, Bobbie and

I — taking a walk after our one o'clock nap — got off the footpath momentarily for two blind people with white probing canes held out as if they were dowsing. As they were, of course, for impediments.

Watching them brought up into my throat the usual humble and apologetic feelings I have in the presence of the disabled, the retarded, the disadvantaged, and I began to feel grateful for my health and competence. Bobbie's upturned face caught my eye; she was watching me.

'What are you saying to me, darling?' I asked.

'Watch out when you feel happy and satisfied and you seem to be OK on all fronts,' she said. 'It may be nothing but fortune fattening you up for its table.'

By the time we'd gone past the phone box and passed down into the Fragrance Garden, walking on the lucky stones set into the path, I'd begun to feel the two blind people were not so much to be pitied, and that my impediments were merely of a different kind.

I wish we'd had time to see, together, all the Niagaras of this earth; the deserts, not missing one; the nervous jungles and their gorgeous inhabitants; the wastes of ice and snow; all the high places; the dozens of seas. (I'll never give up hoping that one day water will feed the world.)

Nothing's Trivial

In my student days I helped with a biology experiment. We volunteers had small colonies of our own skin-mites marked with coloured dyes; the experimenters charted their progress from pore to pore, their migrations, the excursions their young made. One tribe, in particular, was written up extensively; they started beneath my chin and in eighteen months were traced to the middle of my chin — two centimetres distant — where there is a small crease, not exactly a dimple.

I guess little creatures like that think each of us is a continent and they discovered us.

Sitting at home today, with Bobbie curled up on the carpet, I meditated on the migration of that little colony whose epic journey started all those years ago in a small oasis of pores beneath my chin, and now, so many generations of mites later, I imagined them as having migrated up my chin, over my bottom lip, round my mouth — in spite of all my swims, baths and showers — and round my top lip, up to my nose.

They were by nature wanderers, looking for a land flowing with milk and honey, though what was honey to them I could never know and what they used for milk was a microscopic mystery. Perhaps they had an Abraham to lead them once, a Joseph to deliver them, and a Moses to steady them and bind them together with a set of laws so they might survive.

I wonder what their landscape looks like to them, Bobbie.

I've seen, as everyone has, electron micrograph enlargements of pores and cells; with that in mind the country through which my little parasites trekked was as rough and hazardous as the mountains of the moon.

The little colony is now settled, in my imagination, in the curl of my nose. A large number of the young reckless ones had ventured too near my mouth and lips and had vanished inside my mouth, their whereabouts unknown — perhaps among the flora in my gut. The survivors have a tradition that the straying generations are still alive and flourishing, having struck it rich in the mining and exploration business. That's one story. Another is that a mountain opened and swallowed them.

My thoughts wandered, my concentration dissolved in relaxation. I may as well tell the whole truth: I slept. Sitting there with my head back against the gold-patterned wallpaper, the film of my dreams showed me the psychiatric hospital at Wistaria Creek, the flowers in September nodding and blinking in the spring rain, dodging sideways to avoid raindrops in their eyes, but still getting hit; the handsome idiot that had clear-eyed moods when he talked everyone in the place into having sex: rooting everyone in the place — doctors, nurses (they did it for therapy, he did it for victory), patients, even visitors; my childhood visits to the sea when the first smell of the water and salt spray was so delightful and so welcome that I sucked it into me greedily; the time several years after university when I dropped a little of my knowingness and easily acquired cynicism and decided that nothing — nothing we did, nothing that existed — was trivial, everything was part of a whole, that everything should be well done, done for its own sake.

My last dream was little more than an irritating repetition of the phrase 'Animals don't wipe their bums', again and again, until I was so annoyed that I was glad to wake up and finish my drink. As I lifted the fluid to my mouth I reflected, in the space of a second or two, that fish not only excrete without wiping themselves (after all, they don't have arms, poor things) but they have to swim through it. And breathe it!

Sometimes my thoughts don't act my age.

Still, if nothing's trivial, everything you do — shut a door, look at a view, listen to a secret — all you do shouts who and what you are. Why shouldn't thoughts be included in 'all you do'?

In that case . . . what of the thoughts I keep having, all these years later, of the times I had orgasms while my darling baby sucked my breasts?

I didn't pursue it. Instead, there came into my mind the picture of the first time I went to my Bobbie's house, the first one she'd had since she left the family home. It was in Potts Point overlooking the naval establishment. We walked together, hand in hand; I remember feeling absurdly young.

My feet couldn't feel the ground under my shoes, my legs seemed to walk with no effort. I was dying to be involved in her arms. My mouth was dry. Someone had written on her door in chalk: YOU LOVE ME.

I did.

In that moment my fear of being with people was as if it had never been.

⌒

Even now I can feel my nipples hardening into erections under my cotton shirt. How we used to make fun of it, we two together! It happened at the oddest times.

Nipplus erectus, I called it.

⌒

At two-thirty this morning Bobbie and I went for a walk up William Street. There's always traffic, and rarely do you look up the street without seeing people walking. Some of the shopkeepers and motor showrooms leave lights on all night. The stainless steel and glass of Goldstein's shop fittings, ovens, urns and tableware gleamed from their half-dark. The banks, newsagents, pawnshop, dark doorways, the pubs, barber's, furniture display, all were as near asleep as anyone could get within sound of the taxis, trucks, security vans, and all the rest.

The neons were mostly still on in Darlinghurst Road; we walked along in the brightness, slowly, there was no hurry, and stopped near the dandelion fountain. I sat down, and Bobbie went over and smelled the surface of the water.

I found myself looking along Macleay Street. It was out of sight, but down that street was the first house of Bobbie's I was talking about.

(I've never told anyone this before, but as I was having her — no anaesthetic, no gas — I kept getting the beginnings of an orgasm. The pains came, the feeling lessened; the pain retreated, the feelings came again. Oh, that fullness in the birth canal! Until the feeling stayed and both merged into a glorious wildness that lasted minutes. As the last of her left me the strength of the feeling emptied out and the orgasm was aborted.)

∽

We got home before four.

I left the windows wide open, the night was still fragrant.

A salt sea wind, coming in, dug into me looking for anything in the way of a soul — and finding some poor frayed thing, lifted it up. I felt as if my own Bobbie passed close by me in that wind, brushing me with her own air that she carries along with her.

∽

Down in the street the level dark.

51

Halfwits, Beggars and Cripples

Wendy O'Connor (why do I find it so hard to take seriously a woman of seventy-seven called Wendy?) came to me asking about tooth abatement, gum disintegration and vaginal stirring: a disquieting assortment. Only in this vale of laughs, Bobbie, could people concern themselves with such ailments.

She had none of them, she wanted to blow off steam. I just had time to get dressed. An hour before, I'd had this irresistible urge to tear off all my clothes. I didn't particularly mean to rip them, but I had to get everything off quick. I guess I did realise I was actually tearing things.

'The city's full of scrubbers!' she proclaimed. 'I'm getting out of this traditional manufacturing dead-end and into the chip business.'

'Is that where the subsidies are now?' I asked. To be human is to be always in a state of development, always with a problem, though what this has to do with the price of fish I'm at a loss to say.

Her late mother, when she was managing director of O'Connor Industries, a chain of related companies, had delusions of democracy and as an example to her workpeople sent Wendy always to state schools; when mother retired, Wendy took over the reins and stamped out any idea of democracy in the workplace. I loved the way people of Wendy's sort would sell factories as going concerns. That meant selling land and buildings plus machinery and staff and labour force with it in the one package. It amounted to selling people.

How naive I am, Bobbie! At my age idealism should have passed like measles, with just a trace left in the blood to make me immune to further infection.

'Jack's as good as his master, they used to say. I'll tell you what: Jack's as good as a bastard! And Jill's a dill! There's no honest day's work now. The workforce is all halfwits, beggars and cripples. The unions run the country.'

'Indeed?' I said. 'I must ask them how they invest the profits of the banks and insurance companies and the oil and mining giants, and how they're going to allocate the tax revenue in the next budget.'

She unheard me, sitting in front of my desk, a proprietor and executive with pitiless cruelties in her eyes.

'If I had my way,' she began, threateningly. She had middle management beneath her, equipped with velvet gloves: they kept the business going. If she'd had more contact with the workforce she'd have been out of business long since.

'You always have your way, dear,' I said. 'There's nothing the matter with you that's worth bothering about, only age: there's no medicine for that and only one cure. I'm not having you using me as a sounding board, you old grumbler. If you're short of cash, sell a factory.' I never go to visit her these days. Once, when I did, she served up a spine-chilling afternoon tea, and after one particularly hard-drinking night, when I crashed there, a grisly breakfast.

'Doc, it's great to sit here and have someone talk to me like I was the shit. Go on, you be the boss and I'll be —'

'I *am* the boss here, Wendy. Now beat it and don't give me any lip.'

She began to laugh. 'It's good to hear you, Doc. No one abuses me any more.'

'Go on, clear the surgery. Back to your slaves. You're all piss and wind.'

She was enjoying it. 'Mum used to talk to me like that,' she gurgled.

'Out!' I ordered. 'You have no symptoms. There's no advice I could give you. Anything I tried to tell *you* in the way of staying alive wouldn't be worth two knobs of goat shit.'

She loved that one. She came every few months just to hear it, it was her favourite expression.

'See you, Doc,' she said. 'You're a little trimmer.'

I liked to think, once, that if she'd been one of her halfwits, beggars and cripples confronted by an owner of labour as hard as she, that she'd have excuses and fear farting from every orifice. But I don't think so, now. Not Wendy O'Connor.

&

She left. I wondered what it must mean to people whose labour was sold. Did they feel that they, their personalities, their very selves, were items in a business transaction? I daresay they did.

When I was younger I used often to feel (does that mean to think?) that such people, feeling so low in the scale of possessions and power, would feel a strong bond of sympathy for each other, a sort of community: a community of misery, if you like to put it at its worst. Since then I've come to feel there is no true community in misery, and I suppose that means no true community in being oppressed. Each person's is usually more than that person can bear; others' misery and oppression is their own and they will have to cope as best they can.

The engineer says I allow myself a little sympathy for others and an occasional chocolate. Fair enough. But she doesn't know of the many kisses I allowed myself while a certain person slept.

The little kid that delivers the papers each morning has at last dropped her habit of knocking on the door. You know how hard it is for me to get back to sleep once I've been woken early in the morning. There's room under the door for her to push in everything but the two Saturday papers I take. I bet the newsagent tells each kid in turn to knock on doors: she thinks everyone in our building is a thief.

The present kid is small and dark with brown gleaming eyes and thick brows; the bundle of papers she carries looks to be almost as heavy as she is. Actually, she reminds me of the look of that dreadful girl at school that stabbed you with the compasses because you wouldn't kiss her.

☞

Oh, my slippery love, you have eluded me.

Cutting It Out

Little old Roxanne Fishbein, when she was an operator in Europe on the international money market, wouldn't have looked twice at the Lover's Arms. She was one of those who manipulated currencies and made economists in many parts of the world scratch their heads and declare there was nothing they could do. Her equipment was a telephone and tables of exchange rates.

She came to Australia with Linda, her Australian-born wife of many years, and got involved in a road accident that affected her brain. She also lost an eye. The brain damage prevented her resuming her dealing in currencies, and she was at a loose end.

They lived not far away and took to coming to the Lover's Arms. She was seventy-two and could remember milk that settled with the cream on top.

'Fishes have no Beins,' she'd say. A great joke, she thought. Her only one, and the girls reckoned she was harmless. Bein is German for leg, Bobbie, in case you didn't know. Or did you learn German in a previous existence?

Linda had been a plumber before she married Roxanne and went to live in Europe. She wasn't much of a drinker — didn't like it — and did a few plumbing jobs to keep her hand in.

The pub's golfers invited Roxy out with them one Sunday and to their surprise she turned up. It was a six o'clock start at Moore Park. They got used to having her with them and gradually took no notice of her. (She had found her level in the group.) That changed on the ninth.

She went into the rough and her ball was found nestling behind a tuft of Parramatta grass. She took a good swipe at it, her five iron hit the tuft, and the force of the jerk as the tuft pulled her iron up short made her false eye fall out. They picked it up, dusted it off for her — sand had stuck to the eye where it was wet — and handed it back very seriously. She screwed it in with wonderful facial contortions and when she had it straight, as she thought, they fell about until the next foursome yelled at them to play on or bloody well get off the course. There were some hard girls around.

They played on, still burbling with overdue laughs. They didn't have it in them, they told me later, to tell her it wasn't in straight. You need a mirror, of course, to check that it looks straight ahead. The trick is to turn your head when you look at someone, and look straight at them, then the eyes appear to be parallel; if you turn only your good eye, all you're doing is providing joy for onlookers.

This accident gave her ideas of being a star at the pub. When she went for a pee, she'd take the eye out and leave it watching her gin. She was so short, strangers took her for a dwarf, thought she was performing, and even clapped.

Leaving it on the counter was only safe when we were there to mind it for her. Lots of people are itching to get their hands on a glass eye.

She put it on the counter once in the butcher's shop for a joke, and women shrieked. The butcher, a large lady with close-set eyes and a cleaver, warned her.

'You do that again and I'll throw the bastard out in the street.'

The shop was in Oxford Street. Palmer Street was near enough to be a possibility, the hill was steep, a long way to the bottom. Roxy wasn't silly, she didn't need another warning.

The engineer contends honest discussion crushes more relationships than silence. My only question is: do they love you, where you are, more than I loved the headlong gaiety of your mornings?

It's a delightful Sunday. There's a sudden brightness in every day when the knowledge of you flames out. That you exist.

Just as I sat down to write, the bell-ringers in the cathedral began to pull their ropes. The sound of bells coming from that brown architecture seems out of character, perhaps because from my window I see always the south, the shaded side. Bells don't often seem to me to keep to a tune, and this time is no exception, though when I get into their rhythm I find less fault with them.

Why can't there be a stone to build with that's white, and stays white? Imagine looking across and seeing that towered shape white in the sun. Even at night it would be seen.

The bells are still clashing violently as I write this — the bell-ringers must have cramp by now — the resonance is piercing, it pushes the quiet air of Sunday into fantastic shapes — spiky, irregular, yet shimmering with colour.

Can you hear them now, as once you did? Remember how surprised you were when I said they sounded as if they were shrieking in fear?

(My little girl of nine in the blue dress with the white bows: I'm here. I exist. I breathe, still.)

Thank God for Glass Eyes

Fights aren't frequent at the Lover's Arms, but old Fishbein heralded the biggest fight we'd ever had. It was the end of the fortnight, everyone had money and drank that little bit extra that little bit quicker.

Roxy is telling the story of her glass eye and the tuft of grass at the golf course and does her little act of taking it out and putting it on the shiny red tiles of the bar. Several strangers look at it, a local woman moves away with a drink.

Three large foreign women with black hair and sort of brown complexions latch onto this, and move closer. No one has seen them before. One's tall and very big, another's just tall, the third is middle height and square with an almost flat nose.

I guess they just looked around and saw a mob of scruffy dolls and drinkers. They were fantastically well-dressed. Perhaps in their country, the scruffy, workaday people don't talk back to the better-dressed, or little ones to big.

However, in their country they weren't. Resist nothing, the philosopher said, but the Lover's Arms didn't hear her say it. This was the City of Women and Cathedral Street and the Lover's Arms and it wasn't a good idea for them to suddenly grab the eye and, when old Roxy tried to get it back, to toss it one to the other so that whichever one Fishbein approached threw it, and didn't have it, and spread her hands wide to show she was innocent. Like you do at school for fun.

The whole bar was onto this, waiting for little old Roxy to get pushed or hit or knocked about. I moved away into a corner and tried to put Bobbie so her head faced away. It didn't work. Whatever I did, her head turned easily back on its hinges towards whatever action there was. Once she looked up at me, and I shook my head. Ivy took her teeth out, wrapped them in her hanky and slipped them in her pants pocket. Linda the TV mechanic closed her tool-box and pushed it over near the wall. Others finished their drinks so none would get wasted. The talk ceased. Gradually the strangers noticed the edge of silence rolling up like a wave. They shrugged and grinned and carried on, but a bit slower as if they'd decided to get tired of this sport, though in their own good time.

One of the girls sitting at the tables by the window onto Cathedral Street suddenly jumped up in disgust and caught the glass eye in flight. She handed it back to Fishbein, who thanked her and went back to where her audience had been. She still had her eye in her hand and was puffing.

To cover an uncomfortable moment one of the strangers suggested a certain thing to the girl who had caught the eye, and when she made no answer — it was quite rude — she called to her, 'Stupid slut!' The girl was sitting with fairly harmless friends, but she was Emma Kirkpatrick's sister. That was the thing.

The word 'slut' carried all over the Lover's Arms and, almost as soon as it was out, Emma was there.

'That's my sister,' she explained briefly. Whack. She had right on her side.

It was chairs and everything. They were mostly ordinary-sized females, but quite numerous, and proceeded to belt Christ out of three surprised strangers. None of the big and rough girls from the pub was there, only Ivy. And Emma.

Emma never got in trouble, she was quiet and sort of ladylike in a hillbilly way. Her hair was naturally blonde, but she dyed it to make sure and it came out like flax. She was a slow talker and seemed to chew her words, as if she wondered how much to tell you. I think she moved her jaws to gain time, she wasn't a quick lass with words. She was one of those strong women that need a good reason to fight or they'll just walk away from trouble. But she had her reason this time and wasn't letting go of it until those bitches had been taught what would happen when they spoke like that to her sister.

Now when you make love or make war, you find out something of love and of war, but first you find out what *you* are made of, and have your nose rubbed in it. The strangers proceeded to do just that. They held out for about seven minutes before going down. When injuries and weight of numbers got the better of them, they picked themselves up and left as fast as they could.

The locals didn't follow, just stood at the borders of their habitations and watched them run. They had a big car, bright red and with fringed curtains over the back window and all sorts of decorations and cushions and swinging dolls and a plastic hand waving.

When they all came back inside, there was Roxy, taking up where she'd left off.

'And when I went in to the post office' — she was back in Africa

in a place where the whites hadn't been overthrown — 'I took it
out and slapped it on the counter and all the blacks, males be it
said, ran like mad. At last they came creeping back and I got my
piece of paper signed. You've no idea of the red tape. Just like India.
They'd been told that when such and such words are on the paper
then you can do such and such to it. But they haven't been told
why the first such and such are needed or how anything on the
paper fits in with the situation it's supposed to cover. The result
is they have no idea of using their discretion. You might just as
well be talking to kids playing O'Grady Says. If that other figure
or signature isn't there you can talk yourself blue in the face, it
makes no difference. You can explain the whole situation: why the
different things are needed on the paper and how it doesn't cover
the situation you've brought to them — but no. The signature is
not on the paper, Mem. I cannot accept it without the signature,
Mem.

'Thank God for glass eyes.'

⟨⟩

There didn't seem to be much damage to the sturdy furniture,
just a few dents and the odd scraps of glass. The pub settled down
to its usual routine.

'I know the sort,' Ivy was saying. 'Go without it for years, then
when she has someone she changes immediately — goes from sad
to happy in one leap — treats the sex activity as familiar and looks
around from her new-found confidence for someone else ...'

Now I wonder, Bobbie, what that was all about. Finding love?
We'll never know. But you can't go prospecting for love, or drilling
for it. It's not an ore you dig out and take away and sell: it's a fruit
you plant. And all love is one love, wherever it is. Whatever the
thing loved. Whether it's mother love, love of landscape, sexual
love, love of books, love of solitude ... Think of a name-word: love
of *that* is the same love as love of God; and can be expressed
sexually, if you like — or not: it doesn't matter.

I'm really big on love, aren't I, Bobbie? Laugh at me, why don't
you! A woman that can't keep a lover, a poor disappointed lonely
thing that cries in her drink, aches every day, hasn't got sense
enough to forget; then, when the tragedy of it strikes her afresh,
she can't be serious but must let it all run away like water into sand
with a casual comment, a flippant remark.

Regrets ...

Regrets are like a bath; the water gets cold, also dirty; one has to remember to pull the plug afterwards.

There. Done it again. There's no hope for me, Bobbie. It *can* be too late to mend. I just hope I don't get so disgusted with myself that I stop eating. Last time it happened I had to make a tremendous effort of will to get myself to begin again.

⌒

Let us resume our rounds. There are always sick to visit.

My engineer is cool as sea smoke. She says she is a creek of running water, not a still pond.

Nine pelicans flew under the Harbour Bridge as four-legged Bobbie and I walked round the harbour side of the Opera House. One by one they landed on the stone wall of Fort Denison, arranged their wings — that were so elegant and powerful when they were airborne, but now folded clumsily, jerkily, around their bodies — put their long beaks and throat pouches solemnly against their chests, and stood staring worriedly into the water. I felt like rounding my hands and soothing their pathetic little lumps of heads.

Apart from shifting their feet, and turning their heads slightly, they made no movements until Bobbie and I were out of sight, walking in the Botanic Gardens.

Were they visiting? Had they been starved out of lakes in the country, then hunted out of their adopted home at Parramatta where they fished the shallows downstream from the weir? But there were dozens at Parramatta; perhaps there'd been a family row, or the group had got too big and clumsy and split up under its own weight.

I walked on, thinking of our holidays on the coast and watching you swim, of presents at Christmas time, and teasing talk of boyfriends, girlfriends, and of love. And saw idle sailors on ships that pass in the stream. I hope they remember to write home.

A Small Death

Yet another Linda — this time Linda Peachey; she's thirty-one, suffers from chin wither, and her family's been in wheat since the 1830s in the south-west of the state.

Linda's a financial therapy guidance officer, and — this is of greater interest to me — has a dear little Maltese pup she calls Gyp — a tiny thing, as small as vermin. Gyp isn't one of her pedigree names, just a pet name, and Linda loves her. But Gyp has to die, having contracted cancer of the colon.

I've been to visit Linda many times to see how Gyp's going — Linda doesn't need human comfort since her family's wealth provides spiritual health and nourishment. When I go to see her, though, it's hard for me to hear much of Gyp; Linda has the proletariat — horrible word — on her mind. After all these centuries of the poor not making revolutions against the rich, why do the rich have the poor so much on their minds?

'Thank God they can find no more reasons why they should be paid for work that can safely be left to mechanical means, no more reasons why they should continue to be parasites on capital. At last they're facing reality. For so long conventional wisdom had it that business was the parasite; but now capital can exist, and grow, without the people, and they're beginning to appreciate it. Now that we are to all intents and purposes without manufacturing of our own, the people aren't needed as consumers, and with mining and raw materials resources and primary industry and its exports, the consumers are elsewhere anyway. We don't need them!'

She looked at me triumphantly as if taking to herself the credit for recent economic and social changes, and daring me to put my two cents' worth beside her wisdom.

'Is she feeling any pain?' I ask.

'She's a thoroughbred.' As if that matters when she's dying. But I am taken to see Gyp on her sick-bed. She has her own room, and a view. There's a daily visit from the vet and she's protected by drugs from the worst of the pain.

Gyp seems to have absorbed some of Linda's pride in her wealth and her family. With Linda the trait of being of a rich family has carried over into her very nature, so that she, and they, are not merely rich in possessions, but wealthy by nature; Gyp seems to view the world from a similar position, and even contrives to look down on me. Bobbie is a different matter, though, and never fails to shake Gyp's frail spirit. She's getting used to the much larger animal day by day, though there isn't much time left to get to be real friends.

'She's going to heaven, aren't you darling?' Linda asks, but Gyp's sleek, wealth-protected soul doesn't need a god.

⬮

Ah, Bobbie! How I seem to love you more now I see this poor little death, made so pathetic by the useless pride the animal has absorbed and cannot help but radiate even while its own body is becoming the death that is devouring it.

We leave the house and the door shuts behind us, a little too loudly. I know she didn't mean anything by it. I stop with my hand on the gate. Of course! That's what troubles me. How could she go on about the poor like that? How could she?

I shut the gate and know the answer. The rich usually never mention money, or only to cry poor-mouth. But she doesn't care. She doesn't mind what she says. She's dying, and fears nothing. She's dying with Gyp, day by day dying a little more, along with the thing she loves.

Perhaps I, too, shut the gate a little more sharply than I meant. (No, I didn't. A sudden terrible desire to jump out of all restraint tempted me to smash gate against gatepost again and again until the thing sagged loose on its hinges. Only by holding myself tightly in was I able to master the impulse. A little violence leaked out: that's what my more conscientious mind noticed when the clang of the slammed gate was louder then it might have been.)

⬮

Bobbie had her paws up on my table, looking out of the window and glancing to one side at the paper in my typewriter. I had started a new page and was at the part where I said 'As if that matters when she's dying'. It was only a few minutes ago. When she saw me look up, Bobbie pointed her head towards the view. Everything seemed the same, the sun bright, the buildings warm, the harbour filled with glitter. Yet not everything.

On the flat pebble-crete roof of the recreation room at the top of the grammar school building a crow was digging its broad beak into a tiny dead body in the guttering and lifting it out to get at it. Several magpies on the roof kept their distance, but stayed near enough to annoy the crow. As I watched, more magpies came, until there were seventeen — I hadn't realised there were so many — and with the safety of numbers, began to harass the crow, moving near, dive-bombing, swooping from the roof of the new building and buzzing the crow, flying just over its head and landing beyond. The crow looked like nothing so much as a good shepherd defending a lost lamb against wolves. They kept it up until the poor crow retreated to the chimney-pot of a nearby roof, hiding the meat in a place that could be defended.

'Clever old crow,' I said to Bobbie. I'd like to believe she agreed.

But I wonder what little carcase the crow treasured, and protected from the magpies.

❧

The daylight gets brighter now in the late afternoon, as it crowns fewer trees and building tops with gold. Then it will suddenly be gone.

Songs My Mother Taught Me

Did you know my mother, Bobbie? Of course you didn't. One of the stories she told me was of one of her teachers. Mother was a ringleader of dissent at her school, and in the course of being ticked off by the Assistant Head developed a crush on her. The first weekend they spent together, mother found her teacher had breasts on her buttocks. Mother found this unusual, but the teacher explained it was simply the way she developed, and the explanation seemed sufficient. Her lovers had to touch and stroke and compress the nipples by putting their arms round her hips. When she had a child she fed it lying down and facing away.

She had an armoured brassiere specially made. The nipples faced slightly outwards, and mostly had a crumpled appearance. Her greatest success with men had been in face-to-face encounters:

the males liked to have their hands down there. But sometimes, by way of a change, to make their entry from the rear, right between the breasts.

But that's enough of men, Bobbie! We can do far, far better without them, can't we? If they saw you, darling, they'd think of nothing else but shooting you. That's how their minds are.

The engineer diagnosed my ego is where my heart should be. She doesn't know how I cherish lifeless things that were hers and feel the passion hiding in a handkerchief and one discarded slipper.

We were walking in the Gardens; we'd come past the rose beds, past the yellow-wood tree, down the gentle slope to the flat before the sea wall. My favourite old Moreton Bay fig stands there; its buttressing flesh, with that slowly-poured look, making deep caves for children to hide in. Bobbie likes to stretch against the trunk, standing on two legs, and exercise her claws. Sometimes I encourage her to leap up into the branches, where she lies with her arms and legs dangling down, as much at home as a bird on a swaying poplar twig thirty metres high.

Safety of the Hexagon

Mary Watson's complaint is pubic rot. She'd been a grocer's delivery girl once and often looked back wistfully to those young days. Twenty-seven now, she had expected to become a social geometry engineer, but her mind had fallen on evil times.

'All my life I've read stuff others have written!' she exclaimed sourly. 'Now it's all vomiting out.' I think she hoped I'd take notes, though I'd given her no reason to think so.

'You're all in limbo!' she shouted at me. 'All of you. You don't

know who you are! Primitive tribes knew their ancestors. The rich
know. They know. You middle millions don't.'

Suffering senna-pods, Bobbie, I thought, we're going to get the
random words treatment. I was wrong. She began a patchwork tale
that had a beginning, an end, and was all muddle.

'I wasn't always leaping ditches and throwing balls through iron
rings, I had my moments of sensitivity. Mother was terrified of
rooms with square corners and for a time I fancied the sharp
corners of a room held uncertain terrors for me. That sounds
woolly, but behind it there's a truth. When I went into the square
corner of a room it was as if I was projecting myself into a situation
of helplessness, the toy of forces I could not question. I felt: If my
body strikes the wall at this angle, I will deflect and hit the wall
just as hard nearby. In a circular room, even a hexagonal one, I
wouldn't. I drew diagrams to satisfy myself I had something to
concern myself about and sure enough there it was in ink on the
paper. A square room has inhibiting corners, all you can do is stuff
furniture into them to take off their edges. A round room's the best
answer, but a hexagonal one, no matter how you hit it, almost, you
bounce out a decent distance before you make contact again. And
then obliquely.

' "The corners of a room are terrifying." I wrote this on cardboard and pinned it high in my room where I could see it from
my bed. I was uneasy that my father would come in and see it and
wonder, but he never did. I did my own room. In ten years he never
came in my room. He got to hear of my phobia from mother and
I told her never to mention anything about me to other people.
He didn't refer to the notice directly, but out of the blue he said,
"Character, in the old-fashioned sense, is necessary equipment to
avoid constant perception of ever-present death. The nurture of
strong and stable character is a strategy to avoid anxiety."

'I thought it was profound then, and only later I realised he
referred to my terror of square rooms. This terror lasted months.
The day I recovered from its effects I saw a mother walking along
the street with one baby in a pusher and another not much older
toddling alongside her, its nappy lowslung and full. The one with
transport was a lady baby, with gimlet eyes. I knew then there were
more terrors in the world than I had ever imagined; more than I
could cope with. So I relaxed, and ignored them.'

She sat there, saturated with recollections, her runaway train of thought pulled up at some station whose name I would never know.

⟷

Bobbie, my dear, life — for everyone, not just Mary Watson — is walking into a desert. You don't know which direction is best, and when life ends you still don't know. But you keep walking: you must.

⟷

Her room-mate, Lesley Courtenay, thirty-four and designer of throwaway food, entered before Bobbie and I got up to go, and seeing us seated, hobbled over on her crutches to stand over us and lecture us in something of the manner of Mary Watson. Her subject today was Empires. She suffered from muscle crumble and was undergoing treatment at a number of clinics.

'Empires have a bad name these days, but they've brought great benefit to the imperialists. You'll laugh at that — all you middle-class, banner-waving vegetarians do — but think a little further. The conquerors learn the secrets of the conquered and benefit from a great impetus to their science and discovery programmes. I use the word "programmes" derisively.' She had an uneven, unpredictable voice.

'Then, because they're large, the empires can spread their gained science over a large area. In the long run, more people are brought in contact with the new discoveries.'

Her voice, firing its bullets, became overpowering. It compelled my attention, and alarmed me. What was it in her that made her spit words and phrases at a person, as if to hurt?

'Now the new imperialism is called internationalism and it's spread by corporations. It's meant to override the old national boundaries.'

She regarded us with a mixture of zeal and contempt, a common enough combination.

'How's your treatment going?' I asked her, to bring the talk down to important things.

'The treatment is flourishing, I'm getting worse.'

'What are they doing for you?' It was a job keeping my own voice steady. Her voice was like — yes, it was like fragments of violence made audible. It stirred in me, it pushed at my own little stock of answering violence.

'How can they learn about health by studying the sick? That's all they do. I get worse all the time my treatment improves.'

'How do you mean: "improves"?' I managed to be me, to keep my voice level, and friendly. Oh please, don't let me break out of my calm! Last time I had an outbreak I smashed *things*, when it was people I wanted to smash.

'Gets more sophisticated. They've got me on injections, physio, counselling, group comparison therapy, normality orientation excursions. But somewhere out there, away from all the professionals, there's a Christ for my malady; someone who has the answer to everything that's the matter with me. A prophet of the next two thousand years, as Christ has been of the last two. Don't forget Christ was a layman, a member of the public.' As she fired her banal words I thought: how did those two live in the same room together?

Then a horrible thing happened. Suddenly she brought the end of her right crutch down on Bobbie's foot. I mean, her front paw. Involuntarily Bobbie let out that fearful, deep, coughing roar that is natural to her, but which she reins in at other times, as if she knew the terror it produces.

Bobbie recovered her composure — her head had gone forward in immediate attack, but she had refrained — her mouth was still open, her lovely pointed teeth white and shining, her pink gums showing, her nose wrinkled back a little in a perfectly understandable snarl; she fixed Lesley Courtenay and her helplessness with her eyes, which appeared to magnify the light coming in at the window — and grew!

I saw her grow slightly bigger!

What an absurd thing to say. A childish wish for her safety — answered on the spot. Yet when I got up to go, to take her from that atmosphere of cruelty and self-regard, her shoulder came to a higher point on my thigh. I'm sure of it.

There were no apologies. I doubt if she of the muscle crumble was aware, even to the slightest degree, of the danger she had provoked. Mary Watson was cuddling her consciousness of pubic rot over on the settee, looking at a spot in the pattern on the carpet that might have been a hexagon. Or perhaps the face of someone who was talking to her.

The odour of self-absorption filled the room, swirled round the curtains, clung to the legs of the record-player, covered like dust the screen of the television set, permeated the clothes of the two young women. I felt I was choking. Come away, Bobbie. Cruelty's catching.

'Goodbye, girls,' I said, halfway through the door. There was not going to be an answer, I knew, but as I looked back I saw the gleam come again in Lesley's grey eyes, making them brighter, almost keen, with a species of delight. She wanted to do it again.

Ah, cruelty, cruelty! Your satisfaction is soon gone — and no sooner gone than we want it again. I shut the door; they were alone; voices began, and got louder. Bobbie and I began to hurry to the gate. For some reason I felt guilty at going, as if they shouldn't be left alone. But what could I do? What could I say? No one argues with a cyclone, or even with a cool southerly on a hot day, though what this proves I do not know.

I can't even take my own tragedy seriously: I can't be a great deal of help to others, I think, particularly if I give up trying. As my mother said, in what one doesn't attempt there's little danger of success. But I visit Lesley and Mary, and perhaps that's a help, small as it is. The routine of it, the habit of getting a visitor, may get them feeling someone cares; after all, it helps me.

My engineer protests she is not an ivory-tower design engineer.

How blessed are the strong, who need no others, whose hides are thick, who never feel the slights and stings that shrivel weaker ones; who laugh at luck, thumb their nose at love, ignore loss; whose heads are always high. The world loves them, sucks at their shadow.

Poor Lesley, poor Mary.

I can see their block of apartments from my window; it is made of yellow brick. Evenings, I see the girl who has visitors every night; the little Chinese kid who is awake and playing until midnight; the one I call Her Grace, who prances and pirouettes and poses although she is alone, never forgetting to peer at any mirror she passes; the Malaysian girl who is always washing up; the woman sitting every afternoon at a typewriter.

On cool mornings smoke comes from the air-conditioning plant. Around eleven a mother hangs out washing on the roof. The two I visited live round the other side of the building. One of the apartments never has its curtains open at night, but you can see the television screen through the fabric.

The life of the yellow building seems to go on as I've known it, nothing seems to change there. Every night the masked flicker of the TV, every night the washing-up girl, every night Her Grace admiring herself or rubbing creams into her cheeks and round her eyes, every night the girl in the top flat comes back from cruising, with a new person in tow: sometimes old, sometimes young.

Perhaps the sameness of this life has in it the elements of a kind of freedom. After all, freedom, for a train, is in staying on its rails and going forwards or back, but never sideways. Sideways is trouble.

I read somewhere that freedom is rare as the song of a flower no one has seen. I don't believe that. I believe everyone has glimpsed it, however fleetingly — even if only in a dream.

Clouds

We were out in the street, Bobbie and I, and striding along, glad to breathe deeply, and met Coral Bree. Everything had to be violent with Coral. Rage was a permanent condition. I wonder if Bobbie knew that, when she held out her paw for sympathy. She stopped, put her rear on the bitumen pathway and lifted up a paw for Coral to touch. She didn't usually do things like that: perhaps she wanted to disarm Coral's rage. How sensitive you are, my warm, bristly darling!

'Poor Bobbie,' Coral said, doubtfully. 'What's the matter?' Looking at me.

I told her where we'd been, and, I'm ashamed to say, complained about those two. The most enthusiastic informers on women are women, I know, but it all just tumbled out: I guess I hadn't regained my balance after the unpleasantness.

'Wouldn't know if you were up 'em,' Coral raged, in disgust. And went on being disgusted loudly about everything she knew of Lesley and Mary, and recalled, it seemed, every time she'd set eyes on them. Her disgust had a fine dusty air about it, as if she lived in a small cloud she could not escape and the cloud followed her around, attached loosely to her head like a scarf, so that it was never out of her sight and others could always see it or sense it; and this cloud consisted of fine particles of disgust. A marvellous instance of mood in its material aspect.

'Just wouldn't know! Amongst those two a knob of ordinary, decent common sense and human consideration would be scarce as rocking-horse shit!' Hers was the sort of anger you don't intend to get over.

Bobbie turned her head away, doubtless despairing of getting a temperate reply. But you don't realise, Bobbie, how Coral has her own miseries. She's a marginal therapies designer and suffers unspeakable agonies from anal corruption.

⌖

Sometimes when I'm gloomy, and remember that my new Bobbie is not the Bobbie I lost, I talk to you both as if you were together in one skin.

Today I say: Bobbie! My far-away Bobbie. I know ambition and engineering consume you and you are a success. I know your every waking thought is work; I know that whether or not we use it, life goes, and so I say: May you never rest, but some day trail clouds of brightness like stars so that mothers will say to their children: Be like that!

⌖

My comforts are more domestic. One of the stockings I use for drying woollens — threading it through the arms to hang them out — once held her foot, her leg, the miracle of her knee. And I have a photograph of her elfin face when she was ten, standing among other children on the look-out at Katoomba.

There's her first teddy-bear, ginger-brown, still with stiff hair, jaw patched where she used to bite him — patched to keep his stuffing in. Teddy has an amber eye with a black centre — but only one.

> *My engineer needs me less than I need her.*
> *I thought she'd have loved me enough.*

There's a spindly, mousey girl that hangs around the pool tables (they tell me she goes outside the City, wherever she can get a game), the sort with looking-down eyes and a permanent half-

smile, hardly ever takes a drink, and I'd been used to seeing her
with a tall girl with red hair and freckles, about nineteen. The little
spindly girl would be pushing thirty-five. I'd seen her, over a few
years, in just about every pub in the area and always with a very
tall and much younger companion. You remember decent old
Steinbeck's Lennie, the huge, childlike friend of small, sharp
George? Well, not really like that, but not too far off from it. She
used the younger girl as a protector, in case she had to face a bad
loser or two, for she was a hustler and lived on the game. I asked
a few questions and they told me she changed girls every now and
then but they couldn't tell me why. That half-smile, that permanent
joke, irritated me. There's nothing in this world amusing *all* the
time. Is there?

She lived on the pool tables, but only just. Her present protector
is tall and dark, with shirt sleeves rolled up tight near her shoulders
and a grubby, rather desperate expression on her face. She has a
long, sail-shaped nose.

*When I die, all this love for her will dissolve out of me and the wind
will take it. Will it blow on some one? And will that other one feel it
and be changed?*

The Magnificat

Off Oxford Street Jean D'Arcy has her primitive office up two long
flights of stairs. She'd just had her thirty-first birthday, and was an
animal mental-health checker. Pet owners consulted her. She
referred to herself on the hand-printed sign as a Pets Psychiatrist,
and no one was going to argue about it. I called up there to have
a few words with her, and partly to see how she was getting on with
her minor case of labial blast.

She had floor space in what was once a warehouse, with iron

fire-escape stairs out the back, a view of the city skyline and some
of the harbour from the naval dockyard to the creamy snail shells
of the Opera House.

Strangeways, her large white cat, greeted me at the door. Jean
had trained him to be an alarm system, for his leap up onto the
low table where a lot of old magazines lay caused quite a noise,
and she came immediately. She picked up the cat, who watched
me, bristled, and extended his claws.

'You silly cat,' I said affectionately. 'When will you learn that I'll
never hurt you?' At the same time I could see Bobbie yawning and
Strangeways glanced down at her mouth, but her eyes came back
to me and she snarled delicately.

'She really hates you,' said Jean with satisfaction. The only sign
of her disability that I could see was a tendency for her to shift
from one leg to the other with discomfort. A painting on the wall
showed multi-coloured birds growing placidly in the green sky,
and flowers flying in fields the colour of clouds.

Joan constantly petted Strangeways, who struggled to escape,
and at last succeeded. Our lives, this afternoon, were revolving
round our pets. The cat bolted for the kitchen, where he jumped
in a practised way onto the table, and drank milk from a bowl. He
was a sloppy drinker. We humans, lately disembarked from primitive canoes and now familiar with spaceships, followed Strangeways, a domestic cat, into the kitchen; Bobbie, a leopard whose
place was probably the plains of Africa, Asia, South America — anywhere but here — sat quietly by the door. Joan hadn't acknowl-
edged her presence, she doesn't really believe others exist in this
world. She and her concerns are alone. The world echoes with her
voice, the rest is silent emptiness from which now and then indi-
viduals materialise in her office and become clients or patients.

She made tea and we sat round the table. Strangeways, having
cleaned up the available food and drink, leaped heavily into her
lap. Joan grunted, a back foot had gone into her lap in a tender
place. She cuddled the cat, kissed its head and face a lot. I dis-
approve of such closeness to animals.

I didn't want to show I was repelled, so I told her a story of a
cat I had when I was a child: Gubby, the Magnificat.

Gubby taught her two young children safety one day, and I
watched. It was at the back wire-screen door of our old house; the

door opened outwards and swept anything off the small terrazzo step that had the foolishness to be on it. Around nightfall, when plates scraped with a fork signalled food, the two boy cats ran and jumped on the small step. She waited while the first opening of the door outwards swept both children off the step. Mother narrowly missed stepping on one.

The Magnificat waited till mother, having put a parcel of rubbish into the bin, walked back to the door. As she was about five metres from it, Gubby went quickly to the step, stood on it, looked round at the approaching giant and stepped smartly down from the step as mother's feet were nearly on it. She was clear and safe as the door swung outwards.

Mother came out next with the cats' evening meal. As mother neared the door from the inside, Gubby was on the step, then hopped off smartly as she was about to open it. On mother's return journey there was no demonstration: they were all tucking in.

Later, the Magnificat went through the same drill when I went in and out. I'd never seen a cat being a teacher before; the whole lesson was laid out plainly for anyone watching. She did it again next afternoon, then after that left them to shift for themselves. One got the message, the other didn't.

☞

I don't think Jean liked that story, it wasn't about her cat. She was glad when we went. On a shelf I saw a row of herbal remedies. I hoped they would help with labial blast, which had a long and respectable folk history.

☞

I'm glad I rememberd the Magnificat, Bobbie, and I'm glad my memory is still up to it. It was good to remember those childhood days so long ago. Do you remember yours, Bobbie? Of course you do, I see it in your quiet, intelligent eyes. Memory makes us a loan of existence, of life itself, and allows us to cling to a past; memory anchors us to a million details with tiny strings that, together, make a strong chain, strong enough to support us our whole life long.

Often when Bobbie and I reach our door at night and I push the key into the lock and turn it and with a second push the door opens inwards, my internal parts lift and gather in eagerness and my heart, ready for acrobatics, stands on tiptoe to get my first glance, after so many hours, of my proper Bobbie's face turning towards me and lips opening slowly and widening into a smile I am eager to catch because it may be one I've never seen before, and when I've seen it and gathered it into me, I know I will have it as long as I live and be able to treasure it and think of it whenever we are apart.

Of course she's not there these days, so I catch my mood before it falls through the floor, and pat my wordless Bobbie a lot, and get ready for bed. It's taking me a long time to learn I'm alone.

❧

But she *may* be back. There's always hope. I want to be here, waiting for her, just in case. If she comes, what will happen to my new Bobbie? Will she be upset? Will she go out one night and not come back? Will she simply disappear as she sits there on her rug, dissolving into the air? Sometimes, when I look hard at objects round me to try to gauge if it's their intention to stay looking real, I catch, out of the corners of my eyes, shadows sneaking away. If only I had something to hold me tight.

❧

A birdlike woman, not above forty, living a few floors down from me, comes home from work at five past five each day. Her first job is to take her two cats up the fire stairs to the roof, where they have a little run in the open. Both cats are female; one is snowy white, the other a dark tortoise-shell; both are very large cats and as shy as they are big.

On a horizontal pipe against the wall, around chest height, there are usually five or six stones about half the size of cricket balls.

I saw the woman today. She'll talk only to people who like cats. I like cats. The white one, Sandra, is in hospital with a head injury, a big gash over its left eye.

There are flats on the same level as the roof. In one lives a retired woman with a terrible temper.

I mention all these things because they fit together. But so far I haven't had the heart to tell the cat-lady about the row of stones. I don't know what it would do to her to know there were people who hate cats, hate them enough for that, hate them enough to injure them with a stone and put the stone back with the others for next time.

Remember your Puss, Bobbie, when he was getting old, how he used to rub up against us, then fall flat on his side, waiting to be rubbed in return? And how, when he died, we buried him, you and

I, just down the slope from the incinerator where the ground was black with old ashes?

Scars My Mother Taught Me

She woke. It was an April night, cold after rain, with the ground still wet and late-summer growth still on grass and shrubs and trees. The moon was brilliant, high overhead, shining on dewed leaves and glossy surfaces.

My father stood above her. Sleep held her, dragged her heavily down into his hollow of the bed. Her eyes were open. Above her, his set, dream-walking face seemed huge and bloated. She shuddered and the movement woke her a little more. Her arms were beside her. She didn't think to put them up to defend herself.

He drew a razor across her throat. It was a thin pain, blood ran down both sides of her neck.

'I love you,' he said threateningly.

'Mind the sheets,' she mildly urged. They were patterned, flannelette, ready for winter. He was too deep in sleep to hear. His eyes reacted to the sound of her voice, but it seemed only to puzzle him, and made his movements uncertain. He walked away, wavering, and put the razor where it belonged.

Later he puzzled, 'I didn't know you had a cut on your neck.'

'A man cut me in the night, when you were asleep.'

'Don't be silly.'

My mother said she just looked at me. I was nine. Next time the scar itched her, she turned to look at me, and seeing me looking back challengingly, she smiled lovingly. She told me once she heard her parents say maybe she had been changed in the hospital. Sometimes when they had been looking at her, then looked away, she could see in their eyes the girl they wished they had. It wasn't mother.

You know how a scar forms sometimes, as if the flesh were a thick mixture of clay that runs slightly? No? Then remember the way the flesh of a tree closes, seeming to pour, round a wound. It takes a long time. Mother's wounds acquired scars, but for her there was no permanent healing, some constituent natural to humans was lacking in her. If she didn't take a regular pill, her scars opened.

Song of Mother's Scars

Verse 1   She had a scar on her hip where she fell on a camera during the filming of *The Sexual Surfer* in her university days.

Verse 2   A scar on her left temple. She'd been drunk, trying to make friends with another drunk at a club in a fit of midsummer sadness.

Verse 3   There was a gash from a football game on the inside of her right thigh. She was a Virgo, and played for Viragos A team; the injury occurred in a game against Aquarian Old Girls.

Verse 4   A dog-bite, halfway up her left thigh. This was caused by the teeth of a boxer dog owned by a high-school maths teacher she had a crush on, a Miss Dowsett.

Verse 5   A chilblain scar on the big knuckle of her right forefinger.

Verse 6   A scar on the back of her left wrist from the time she worked in a sheet-metal factory on a work experience holiday.

Verse 7   White scars on her palms when she'd gone swimming round the rocks on a northern beach. She dived into a rock pool at the sea's edge; the sea sucked, and she landed on a pool bottom spread with broken bottles left by carefree people on holiday.

Verse 8   Scars on her back and ankles. I don't remember the words of this verse.

Chorus   All her scars opened if she forgot her tablets.

When I was a girl, I've seen her, after being a little drunk for a day or two, staggering round with open wounds, trying to find and pick up her plastic bottle of tablets with hands covered in cuts. Once when I was twelve, I saw her trying to pick it up, and not able to direct the lip of the bottle away from the opened wounds. The lip lodged each time inside a trench of opened flesh.

It was strange seeing the flesh open without bleeding.

&

When I was thirteen, faced with a winter plateful of porridge that I saw as a thin white sea with mysteries in its depths that I had no wish to discover, I bargained with her: I would listen to the song of the scars if she would let me off eating my boiled oats. She made a sudden movement towards me with her hand and I ran out of the house. Perhaps she didn't know she was holding the bread-knife, the one with the wavy edge.

'You ought to be ashamed of yourself, talking to your mother like that,' she said. It always made me uneasy to hear her speak of herself in the third person.

We lived out in the suburbs then; mother was a landscape deformation engineer. I hadn't yet begun the habit, in moments of doubt and not knowing what to think, of tearing off my clothes. That is comparatively recent. And I mean really tearing. I don't know where the impulse came from; no one in the family did it, and none of my acquaintances.

My engineer warns that what's bred in the bone comes out in the flesh, so though I'm defeated I won't go under. I'll never make mine the slavish meekness and submission advocated by that Great Defeated, that Galilean.

This morning I saw the caretaker and her Corgi out for a walk. They'd been through Hyde Park and had gone along Liverpool Street and the caretaker was walking down Yurong. The Duke wasn't. He was on the corner, facing down Liverpool, saying as plainly as could be said: 'I want to go *that* way.' The way the care-taker was headed, home was only two blocks away, and her companion wanted to double that distance, at least. She kept walk-ing down Yurong, head turned away, then stopping, giving the Duke time to change his mind, relent, and catch up. The Duke turned his head slightly to see where she was, then resolutely faced the way he wanted to go, like the prow of a ship.

I didn't see the outcome. As Bobbie and I were about to go up the mock-marble steps of the building, we looked back and saw that things were just as they'd been, except that the caretaker was a little further downhill. The Duke stubbornly faced the detour. Even if he didn't get to walk that way, he was still prolonging the freedom of the walk, postponing the time when he'd have to go back within four walls.

If only others could see us together, still. These people round here, who don't know me, how they'd love her! They'd think altogether differently of me, knowing she was mine.

Old Man Death

The hunters of youth are not the only threats to the City of Women; besides hostile and aggressive males on the outside, there is now Old Man Death. He uses not a mythic scythe, but his own sexual weapons: first an immobilising dart, the type vets use; a sharp knife to open the flesh of the female; the penis to bury a depth charge of semen into the terrible wound. The last element of the attack is closing the wound with needle and thread.

Some christened him the Meat Murderer, though he hadn't killed yet: most call him Old Man Death.

His first victim was Jacqui Chilvers, a nutritional waste notifier and garbage analyst; I'd advised her where to get treatment for anal pus. Old Man Death tranquillised her, cut into her right buttock, deposited his microscopic bombs and sewed her up with an ordinary darning needle and black Sylko thread. A note left in her hand read:

> 'No one can see what I see
> No one can feel what I feel
> No one can know what I know
> I am the only one that is me.'

⌒

Sergeant Appleton, desk sergeant at Darlinghurst, had just joked with a barrow-woman outside Ansett, taken an apple off the display and was headed back to the station. Walking past Foley Lane in her lunch hour, she discovered Jacqui on the back seat of a stolen car. She told me privately she was going over and over in her head the words spoken that morning in a lecture given in College Street before senior police, social workers, politicians and medical researchers: 'Our need is for a cheap and simple way to control an emerging non-working class', when this sight confronted her. Jacqui was in Casualty in ten minutes and the note was being analysed. It was the most interesting case the sergeant had known, and it was dropped in her lap just like that.

I must admit, Bobbie, there is a certain originality, even a degenerate glamour, to the crime. But we must see that you are never in range of those darts. Or me either.

Up to now the City of Women has been the only place a woman could walk with her leopard. Please may it stay that way!

She cruelly advised me to take up growing plants in pots — 'or grow a rose in your heart'.

We loved each other and it was one love. Now it's separate and still only one.

Bobbie is asleep on her rug, the sun slants in at the window; only a metre or so of carpet is alive with light, it's not like the sun of June, July and August, when the sunlight reaches almost to the far wall. The northern shore across the harbour is blue-grey with haze, mysteriously dark with the sun behind it; only a few dozen roofs, out of thousands, show a reflection. The skyline is irregular with trees and lumpy with tallish apartment buildings. The glitter of the sun on the water is brilliant and so fierce you have to look away; the cathedral buttresses are edged in gold, the Domain trees dark. My eyes take a rest from all this stillness and colour. I look round the white walls of my room, at the green carpet, pale as winter grass.

On the carpet in the shade, doing no harm, is a large cockroach. There are so many in the City. How do they make a living? I leave no food around, though once or twice I've caught them shopping around on my cupboard shelves. This one is very big and shiny; he's been encouraged to come out by the general air of sleepiness.

'You won't find anything here,' I tell him; and Bobbie stirs slightly and settles her head at a different angle. The cockroach takes no notice. They never do. I call them the little brothers of the poor.

The Apollo Orgy

He was a captured male. The first time I saw him, in the back of a warehouse in Norman Street, he had a muddled-looking penis and worried feet, yet they assured me he would be all right on the night. Which night? I went down the hill to the Lover's Arms to find out. How could they think crude reprisal was a way to combat our everlasting enemy?

❧

Ivy had given a new roomer at the pub a casual invitation to have a drink in the bar any time. When I walked in, there they were, and the new tenant pouring out woe.

Ivy looked relieved as I set my drink down, hitched up my pants to make the waist comfortable, sat and lifted my glass with its tiny beads of condensation on the outside, took a nearer and nearer look at the bubbles in the white froth — starting from a few big bubbles of about five millimetres, going down in size to bubbles so small that you can only see the froth as a white surface — took a mouthful, swallowed, relished the taste on my tongue and all round my mouth, and licked my lips.

'Yeah, go on,' Ivy said to the tenant as they both finished watching me enjoy my first mouthful of the day. Out of the side windows I saw clouds, high up and massy, a touch of grey underneath, and fiords in the clouds.

'I was there on my Tod, painting this house. It was a sunny day and a big two-storey place, worth two hundred thousand then. A hot day and I was burning the old paint off with a blowtorch, sat

down for a spell, lit a smoke, finished it, shut my eyes for a second
or two and left the blowtorch on. It was hard to get going.'

She made jerky movements with her hands, which didn't seem,
as gestures, to fit the story she was telling. Her hands reminded
me of the black bats that fly from the Gardens and the Domain,
south to the wide spaces of Centennial Park. They flitter heavily
towards my building, dipping and dodging, and sheer off from my
window at the last moment, and go past for their fruit and other
night prey. Her voice went on.

'Next thing, I hear this roaring. Open my eyes. The house has
caught. A few kilometres outside Lithgow it was. No one anywhere
around to give me a hand, and the phone to call the fire brigade
is inside the house. Couldn't reach it. Ashes, just ashes.'

'When was this?' asks Ivy.

'Eight years ago. Still paying it off.' And her hands signed off,
clumsily, in mid-air, falling in disarray to her lap where they lay
like two dead birds in a heap.

If we hadn't broken up the conversation just then we might
never have got to the orgy. The woman was all set to go on for
hours — you can spot the type if you've spent time in taverns and
such places.

The local bowling club committee was looking for funds. All
on the quiet, mind you. They'd blackballed the Lady Lover, a large
girl with sexual ambitions, and others of the girls in years past
when they went mad and had a shot at joining — the club didn't
want fighters and larrikins in the place, ladies or not, but they knew
the place to come when they wanted a sex night. My very word.
They were nice as pie to Ivy.

On the way home I stopped to read in the park. Bobbie had fun
chasing some butterflies, running and springing into the air
delightedly, snapping her teeth and missing the elusive wings.
Others rose from the grass and Bobbie seemed to be pretending
to be undecided about which one to catch, and happily caught
none.

They held the night up the hill in the double garage of a large,
newly built house. Plenty of room for the keg and the mats for the
exhibition — borrowed tatamis from the martial arts club — but
standing room only for the paying audience.

Are thoughts objects? I'd thought when I saw the captive male
that this was a poor specimen, so much so that I'd have been pre-

pared to swear he was no damned good for this sort of thing. I was so convinced I was right that the certainty of it was like a fixed lump of knowledge in me, a lump I could touch and handle. I was wrong.

He came out stripped, with a body like the Apollo on the Archibald fountain. His penis was like the ends, the new growth, that you see on thick, succulent spring plants. I've lost my taste for it these many years, but it brought to my mind straightaway the body of my Gordon, from years ago. How many times, Bobbie, have I wished, in weak moments, that his body had been with me? His body that carried the essence of his maleness. (I shudder when I think of those times we made love, before Bobbie came, and he'd be trying to do it a second or third time, rasping away and sweating rivers, and I'd say, 'Darling, haven't you slimed *yet*?' Heartlessly, and thinking it a great joke. Poor Gordon. He was faithful, I'll say that for him: he started a love affair with himself in adolescence and it's still passionate. And he wonders why I told him to go.)

Apollo came out on tiptoes, almost dancing.

'I want a volunteer,' he says. No one volunteers, so he tries to stir up a few of the girls closest to him.

'Everyone two paces back,' says Ivy. 'I'll volunteer.' And a curious sigh went through the audience.

'Fair enough,' says Apollo. 'Get your gear off and down on the mat.'

She does this and he gets her to lie down with him in a sixty-niner. She has a big view and something to do with her hands.

'I'll try and resist you,' he says, and Ivy goes to work. Goodness me, Bobbie, it's years since I've seen this. Long before the City of Women.

Apollo resists like mad, sweating with the effort, and all the time she's stretching it and doing all sort of things. Apollo's muscles stand out, the veins on his forehead bulge up. In order not to let it happen he takes his head away from her naked lap. But he's in the hands of an expert. Finally he gets a little joey; then, bit by bit and throb by throb, a roaring great stiff. She gave it no rest and judged the moment nicely. When it erupted, her mouth was off it, and the audience got the full effect. After the display, ignominy set in, and it wilted to great laughter.

Several of the females who until then had thought men had

three heads were noticed to be quieter and ready to believe they had only two.

For his next turn Apollo got everyóne stripped. Even Georgina, and that was something. I was beginning to believe, Bobbie, that when they said women criminals with guns had hi-jacked him they were straying slightly from the absolute truth. He was too practised. They'd hired him.

'Gear off, girls,' he said. The place was a mess. Shirts, shoes, pants, jeans, socks, even a few brassieres, over the floor, hanging from the keg and on the drinks table among the wines. And a crowd of women bare and feeling funny, but game.

He looked round at the bodies, but nothing satisfied him until he clapped eyes on Linda the TV mechanic. If he was Apollo, she was a female Hercules. Muscles and curves stood out everywhere, yet she wasn't fat.

'Her. You,' he said rudely. 'What's your name?'

'Meataxe!' the young ones roared. It was news to me. From the expression 'mad as a meataxe' I daresay. Or had she been involved in those daredevil raids into enemy territory, when males were damaged?

'Apollo and the Meataxe,' he said aloud, thinking, and smiling like the cat from Cheshire, not taking his eyes off her. He had rested, and his penis rose, commanded doubtless by Linda.

'Ah,' he said, and got Linda down on the mat and into position. I swear her apparatus looked like the mouth of an octopus. They went about it, but instead of him having as many as wanted it, he stayed with Linda, and began to make her a proposition. She told us later it was about travelling round with him to the various businessmen's clubs and RSLs and Leagues clubs in the outside world where he had his sex shows.

'Give 'em something to talk about, you will,' he whispered. 'Go on, be in it. Have a lash. You'll make lots of money if you get out of here, away from all this.'

'I'm not interested in bucks,' she said she told him. 'I work, I have all I need.'

'What're you comin' at?' he hissed in her ear. She said it tickled.

In the background some sort of argument broke out. Ivy was in it.

'What's the strong of you?' Apollo said to Linda coarsely. 'Don't give us the shits. 'Course you're interested in bucks, that's the name of the game. That's where it's at.'

I heard Ivy's voice. 'I won't tell you again,' she said to someone.
I watched the act. Apollo was angry. He pulled away a bit. Linda
didn't mind. She rested there.

'What *is* the key to you, anyway?' He changed tactics, slid back
into her. 'Come on, you're a great sport. Real great. You could get
out of it any time you liked. Just a short contract, then if you liked
the life, away we go again. It's a great business, show business.'

But events were closing in on their little conversation. Ivy
suddenly swung. I heard the soft thock of her big fist where it took
someone on the side of the face and pushed the jawbone sideways.
I took Bobbie away through the thinner part of the crowd as quick
as I could — emotional troubles communicated themselves to her
and she got excited. I wasn't sure I could hold her if she wanted
to join in. I craned my neck round to see as I was going away; the
two on the mat were still horizontal. But not for long. I guess Linda
didn't fancy being on the ground when bodies started falling
around. Anyway, the woman Ivy hit must have fallen against someone else, because the someone else gave her anothery for good
measure and she went all the way down. Ivy's elbow perhaps grazed
someone who didn't appreciate being grazed, because whoever
that was got stuck into Ivy.

It was on.

Linda brought both arms up against the bottom ribs of Apollo,
and pushed him off with ease. It came out, dripping. She stood
up, bare like the rest and prepared to defend her front.

A neighbour made the mistake of coming and telling us she'd
rung the police because of the noise — after all, drinks *had* been
taken for some time before the main show — but when certain
warnings were transmitted in her direction by members of the
audience, rather hard ladies in the reputation business, she waited
out the front till the police came, to withdraw the complaint. If
she'd done the usual sneaky neighbour trick she'd have got us all
caught. (We'd elected the city council, but we didn't know then
they'd be such wowsers. We know now.) As it was, we had time
to get dressed.

The Lady Lover, one of the girls who'd been in and out of jail
a lot, and very scared of police ladies because of her record, tried
to make things safe for herself by taking a Vincent's powder. This
brought her out in red blotches: she was allergic to powders. For
good measure she dipped a few of her hairs, the hairs of her head,

into the edge of her eyes. This brought her eyes up, puffy and angry. She was allergic to her own hair.

The police, who decided to have a look anyway, were confronted at the door by this leper, and behind her was a crowd of respectably dressed but oddly knocked about women of all ages. They hid Apollo behind Ivy.

The Jills nodded their heads and went slowly back to the paddy wagon. Something was on, but they couldn't put their finger on it. One of the coppers was McRitchie — Angela McRitchie — who once used to piss up with the girls and take part in gambling nights and fix traffic blues. Somewhere along the line she got religion or promotion or something, because now it was 'Get out! Piss off!' and she didn't want to know you. They stayed out there watching a long time.

Inside the double garage they were all working like mad at being good friends. Apollo was sitting on Ivy's knee. She towered above him, showing him how to make a right cross.

Soon as the paddy wagon left Apollo got his money and hurried away to his car — more deceit! — deaf to all pleas. He'd given Linda up as a waste of time. He had a does' night to go to in Foveaux. He loved bucks.

On the way home the bottles of the milk truck chimed a new day and life continuing.

Oh Bobbie! What do you think of Billie Shockley now? Inventor, engineer, creator, exploiter, failed lover, failed friend, voyeur. The one who proclaims: 'Only women here! This is a women's world!' And what did she think of, tonight? If only his body was with me now ... But no. That's all gone. There's only empty space where Gordon was. I've always felt my fate to be fluid. I got rid of him to give all of myself to Bobbie, to reality. And the real Bobbie ran away. The first Bobbie, I mean, darling. Tell me to shut up if I mention the name Gordon again, won't you, Bobbie!

She said I cried out to be ignored; said I'm a poem written in a hurry. No one else knows what it is I had, but I lived it: I know. Where is a doubting Thomas to poke fingers in my wounds? For I have them. Here they are.

On the way home out of Victoria into William, I saw the tiny lady that goes out to the crematorium every fortnight to mourn her lost little boy. He ran away when he was eleven and the way it is in her mind he's dead.

He's not dead; he's a giant of a man, twenty-two now and one of the up-and-coming thugs in the suburban club business, being groomed for executive rank in an organisation.

The tiny lady touches lovingly the bronze plaques in the Wall of Remembrance each fortnight, but also remembers her little boy every time a plaque catches her eye.

As I walked past with Bobbie on her lead, the tiny lady was touching reverently the small bronze name-plate quietly advertising the presence of Gordon F. Crook, Dentist. Her fingers lingered on the emergency after-hours number.

'My darling boy,' she said, so late at night. 'God bless and keep you. My darling son.'

I looked back a bit later and she had moved on to an Estate Agent's name-plate, still loving her lost little boy.

She reminded me of me.

Joker in the Pack

I'd got over my first panic at the thought of having to be with people today, and I was taking Bobbie for our Saturday morning walk. I took little notice of the crappa-crappa-crappa sound of the helicopter. When the papers began to flutter down around us I remembered, and looked up, but it had gone. The papers read: YOU NEED LOVE and I NEED LOVE — no other marks. Some ineffectual male trying to undo the effects of past hostility. How clumsy they are, Bobbie.

At the Lover's Arms, Ivy was talking to big Wheeler, the footballer. Mary Wheeler was one of the new breed of older athletes, one of the first generation of serious football players, but now over the hill as far as top district teams were concerned. We hadn't had any ladies over forty in our local football team before. What with the grog and children and so forth, all the kids that went up through age football ranks to senior football and to grade standard were past it by twenty-eight. The dedicated ones sometimes went to their early thirties.

She wasn't all that good on the field — the standard has gone up so much now — it was just that she never seemed to get hurt. Kicks, trodden hands, chipped elbows, a pile of players on top of her as a scrum collapsed, head collisions, knees kicked: it was all the same to Mary Wheeler.

On the field some urger would yell, 'Wheel it to Wheeler!' and the pass would get folded in close to the ribs, overhung by her muscular-looking bosom, she'd put the head down, and up the field.

'Up the guts, Wheeler!' supporters shouted in voices fogged by drink.

She never got far. Her speed was down, though she wasn't slower than most of the other forwards. The opposition would gather round trying to pull her down, and that's how it ended up. They got her down and it was always in a great pile of bodies. She'd go a distance with three or four on her back and clinging to legs and waist and wouldn't consent to fall until someone got her knees together and held them that way. Momentum did the rest. Sometimes the fall was slow, like slow-motion film of buildings going down.

'If you get up quick, you'll be in time for the old-age pension,' some wit would yodel. She never snapped at things like that.

∾

Ivy was talking, Wheeler listening. 'And as she flashed down past the various floors of the Empire State Building she was talking to herself and a cleaner on the second floor distinctly heard her say "All right so far." '

I gave the old joke its due in a kind of chuckle, but Wheeler didn't laugh at all. Ivy was trying Wheeler out, seeing where her funny-bone was. Seeing I reacted, Wheeler pulled her battered face up a bit at the cheekbones so that a crease or two reached down towards the corners of her mouth and lifted it a little. Her eyes were still puzzled.

'She wasn't all right a second later,' I said, prompting. Still no smile. Ivy looked triumphant, as if she found what she was looking for.

∾

On the back of Wheeler's right hand was a tattoo: $5000, it read. She'd got it put on in Oxford Street when she was a young larrikin and someone dobbed her in for something nasty she'd done and it cost her five grand.

'Never trust anyone with money,' she said when she was almost through her ninth schooner. Always drank beer. It was always nearly through the ninth that she remembered. That was one way you could tell how many she'd had. If she said it almost through her second, you knew she'd had seven before, somewhere else. Apart from that, you'd never know she'd been drinking. Until all of a sudden she'd disappear. Had an automatic cut-out; when she was full, she'd go for a pee and vanish. Probably make it home, then pass out.

She had scars everywhere — face, neck, chest, arms, hands, legs. And movable lumps of bone on her elbows and knees. When she showered after the weekend game, there was a ring of silver hair round both nipples. I notice nipples.

She went away for two minutes. Ivy said, 'She respects you.'

'What game are you playing now?'

'And you're beginning to like her,' she said. 'But which came first?' She wanted me to ponder this. I shook my head.

'You're going to be disappointed. I'm not playing that game.'
She shrugged.

A well-wisher brought over a slice of watermelon for Bobbie. I nodded permission and Bobbie licked the watermelon, but had no interest in eating it. This was hard to communicate to the well-wisher, but finally she took the slice away and put it in with the rubbish.

∽

Mary Wheeler had the stump of an old tree in the backyard of her little house in Forbes Street and every time she went to burn it out it either rained or there were fire regulations — too near the fence, or something.

If it was fine weather she'd ring the fire station to make sure it was all right to burn off. OK, they'd say. Then, just as she was about to ring off they'd amend it to: *Should* be OK. When it was nicely burning, the district fire officer would ring, a fire truck would scream up and start playing hoses on the flames.

After eight goes at it she gave up. The stump's still there along with the rubbish she shots round it.

'Forget it,' she said. 'Bugger 'em. If they stop me every time, they can look at the bloody thing for ever as far as I'm concerned.' As if 'they' cared.

She used to think it was a hex put on her: actually it was her liking for practical jokes that did it.

She never woke up, yet she'd told me a story from which I guessed who it was that was doing this to her.

'It was with our bush-walking club at Colo, near the river,' she was telling me after their game with Dundas. The whole team had limps or cuts inside the mouth or dried blood on knees and knuckles every time City played Dundas. (All the bastards outside the City called us by our initials, but I won't lower myself to spell them out.) But the Dundas girls were good guys. Everyone said so.

'We were camped one night in our two-man tents under a crazy big tree. We had the best spot in the whole group. When I woke in the morning and stretched out, there was something hard that my feet rammed into. It was only the biggest branch of the tree, fallen across the end of our tent.'

She took a suck at her schooner, the level fell five or six centimetres. I used to drink quickly when I was younger, I've slowed now. It's not that I've gone off it: I like it more.

'But we were well off, the bushy end of the branch had flattened the group leader's tent. She couldn't move. Not hurt, just pinned to the ground. She had to sing out a while before anyone lifted it off her. And it *was* a long while. We were all deaf. But she knew I was in the next tent and after that she always tried to get me for little things.'

Maybe Wheeler went out early each morning, or later, or always came home a different time from Baker, the ex-youth group leader. You can live two houses or a street away, in city or suburbs, and never see who lives in such and such a house. Unless on the weekend she happens to be out front just when you happen to look.

But it was Baker all right. I'd seen her going off to do her morning, afternoon and night shifts at the fire station. It had to be Baker. She'd word them up that any time Wheeler asked about having a fire, they'd fix her with the fire truck. The incident with the fallen branch had made an impression on both.

❧

Wheeler had a job outside the City of Women for a while as a security guard, the sort of job where you look at dockets all day and make patrols round the works at night, and time sometimes hangs pretty heavy.

She thought she'd play a joke on Tick Tock, her male fellow-worker on day shift and a person obsessed, for some reason — possibly genetic — with clocks. They needed two of them on day shift to handle the in and out traffic, looking under vehicle seats, in toolboxes, in boots of cars, checking that not too many company assets went out with each vehicle.

One young guy in business for himself used to take full drums of industrial cleaning liquid on to the site and empty ones away. Drums were ideal for taking out company products, which also were liquid.

Wheeler looked at the young male's documents and went over to the drums. She tipped most of them by hand to see they were empty, but the last one she touched didn't move. She tried to wrestle it, couldn't budge it, then put both arms round it and just succeeded in tipping it off balance and allowed it to right itself. And stood back, wiping her forehead at the exertion. Then she took a sneaky look round, winked at the young guy, shoved the papers into his hand quickly and stood back so he could get away.

Tick Tock saw this, and being a man who put the good of the company before loyalty to mates or to other people's rackets, shot over and grabbed the young guy, took the bits of paper off him and ran his finger down the list.

'All empty?' he said triumphantly, and turned to the heavy drum at the back. 'We'll see about that.'

He stuffed the despatch dockets in his tunic pocket — they were done up like the military with brass buttons (though the brass in their pay was light on, the uniform was a sort of compensation) — put both arms round the heavy drum and gave an al-bloody-mighty heave.

His body straightened, the drum flew up and up, over his head; the momentum of his heave was too great to stop the drum: it smashed into the blue painted steel eaves of the gatehouse, caught an edge, and bounced down the armoured glass windows, leaving an impact mark from which radiated three long cracks. It was the sort of glass with wire laminated inside it.

The drum was as empty as the others. Wheeler had been acting. The young guy wasn't about to be caught like that, his racket was tools. Always came in with old, beat-up tools and went out with new. No one on the gate noticed this. He ran an exchange service: tradesmen with old tools gave them to him and he'd exchange them for company issue tools he'd pick up in places he went to, charging a fee like any reputable business man.

Tick Tock was ropable. Right out there in the open like a shag on a rock he couldn't do anything, he had to wear it. (He'd have got a surprise if he tried to fight Mary Wheeler.) The personnel office was one side of him and the manager's office the other. He bided his time.

He took to carrying a camera in his pocket, and as soon as Wheeler weakened one afternoon on a weekend when there was nought to do, and leaned back in her chair and had a snore, Tick Tock snapped a photograph and sent prints in to the office.

Wheeler left shortly after.

◔

None of this cured her of practical jokes.

At her next job she got on one of the emery wheels and used a piece of soft metal on it. That is, she'd pretend to be grinding some brass or copper or white metal. Everyone knows soft metal clogs the pores of an emery wheel and the clogged pores heat up and eventually the wheel explodes. It must happen.

Wheeler had to do things like this. Once she knew a certain thing could be done and produced an interesting result, she had to do it. She showed the young kids how to do it, female apprentices and all. After she'd been at a small, metal-working establishment at Silverwater for a while, they went through an emery wheel a week. Until Wheeler went.

Changing jobs didn't trouble her. She had kids, but you'd never know it, she was always at the pub. And on Sunday at ten in the morning after a heavy Saturday night, lining up outside the club with the Sick Parade.

There was a party at Ivy's place in Liverpool Street to farewell Terry, from the Worker's Arms up the street. It's only fair to mention that Ivy paid for it herself; the girls thought they were doing her a favour turning up and drinking her grog.

On the night there was that little thing the matter with the keg that will happen now and then; the beer was just a little bit off, and had a dramatic loosening effect on the guests.

It didn't work till they were well on in drink, so they didn't mind much. Wheeler wasn't affected, nor was I. She got entertainment watching the afflicted try the toilet, find it full, then race off towards a patch of ground near the back fence. We both noticed how many strange faces there were enjoying Ivy's beer. One that went past clutching her stomach made Wheeler's eyebrows go up. 'That was Baker!' she said. 'I've never seen her down the pub.' Wheeler's trouble was she never left the pub.

She was off like a shot, over to Ivy's toolshed. Baker was still in sight, walking earnestly, when Wheeler appeared with a long-handled shovel and went off after her old group leader, keeping to the shrubs and trees.

I kept my head down and followed in the darkness, taking refuge in a big bush against the side fence. Wheeler didn't make a sound; she crept up behind Baker and extended the shovel from behind a thick may bush so the blade of it poked under the squatting white bottom. When the load was deposited on the shovel, Wheeler withdrew it carefully. Baker half straightened and wiped herself with a piece of newspaper and a tissue, but when she performed the most common and easily understandable action of all — that is, when she looked down and round to see what she had done before putting the paper on it like a blessing — there was nothing.

She looked round the other way, as if perhaps she'd misjudged the angle. Nothing. She went round in circles within a metre or two radius of where she thought it ought to be.

Amid the encircling gloom, Wheeler didn't move. I didn't move. Baker increased the radius. Nothing.

She still had the paper in her hand, with nowhere to put it. She searched everywhere. At last she pulled her pants up, made a sad little hole in the earth and buried the paper by itself. I'd never understood before how necessary it was that the paper accompany the pile.

We followed Baker over to the keg and watched her. She didn't speak to anyone, beyond getting a beer, for fully ten minutes. Then she saw Wheeler. I saw in her eyes that she was immediately transported back to that tent in the Colo wilderness, pinned to the ground.

I walked away to talk to Ivy, wondering what new bastardry Baker would think up for Wheeler.

The yard was enclosed. I'd let Bobbie be by herself. When I next saw her she was playing near the side fence with a terrified rat. It was large, as rats go; all the more flesh to shake with fear. I called

Bobbie away, so as not to draw attention to the presence of rats. Besides, I didn't want Bobbie picking up something nasty from it.

She told me once that I was neither shit nor grit.

Night is coming on, the city buildings are dark blobs hollowed out by lights, the pink and green and gold of the sky on the northern side of the harbour are losing colour to an evening grey.

It was a night like this I saw the old *Arcadia* leaving Sydney for the last time, on the way to Hong Kong, then to the ship-breaking yards at Taiwan.

It was an afternoon I saw last the *Betelgeuse* in the stream on the way down the harbour, some weeks before it burned on the other side of the planet. The shipping notices in the paper mostly spelled the name 'BETEIGEUSE'. I wonder why? Perhaps the paint had come off the bottom of the L on the bow of the ship.

The *Fairsea* and her sisters, the Russian cruiseships, the *Minghua*, the new P&O liners, I see them all, sailing towards the Heads, lights on, where the harbour comes floating between the Heads. My only complaint is they don't keep their funnels lit up and illuminations on till they're well out to sea, at least.

When the *Arcadia* left, around seven forty-five past Garden Island on that January evening — the 29th — I could see the people lining the cliffs on North Head — through my binoculars, of course — and I was sad that a piece of the world I knew was going and not coming back. Not ever coming back.

The Old Woman with One Tooth

She began to sneeze as I opened the door of the Lover's Arms. One, two, three . . . She got to fourteen, and the way her head lifted, with

that dreamy, tranced look, I could tell she was good for many
more.

'Stop!' I commanded. She turned slightly to look. Her face was
a network of wrinkles like a delta where many water courses once
ran, but now are dry. 'It was interesting to begin with, Cynthia. Put
a lid on it.'

She was still for a bit, trying to gather herself for another sneeze,
then the moment was past.

'You stopped my sneeze,' she complained, but she seemed
pleased to see me. I'll never get over being amazed by how nice
people are to you if you see them rarely enough.

Cynthia would be seventy-seven in the shade and gone in the
shanks, but years ago was the terror of East Sydney. She took over
from old Hourigan; they fought at the bottom end of Glenmore
Road, outside the oval, and the battle went sixty rounds. She was
now like old Mother Time, sucking at the blood of youth; at the
end of each drink you could see her grinning at some private joke:
she was fit to carry on forever. Her skin was loose and wrinkled,
but you can tell when she was younger she'd had, as they say,
muscles in her shit.

She became a pro wrestler, and met most of the great ones —
the Russians, the Swedes, the Maoris — and when she wasn't
wrestling she was chucker-out at the local dances, clubs and discos.
She'd spot some infringement or trouble starting and she'd go into
the fray with joy in her heart.

I liked to listen to her stories, so once she brought her posters
and photographs from the old days, stories about her seven-
hundred-and-fifty-pound deadlift — what's that? Three-fifty kilos,
near enough? How she lifted the front ends of cars, and the time
an iron slab table was left by the crane driver in a position where
the foundry employees couldn't get at their sheet steel and she
lifted it behind her back, it was so heavy. None of the men could
move it.

'I did you a favour,' I replied in answer to her sneeze complaint.
'More of that caper and you'll have a heart attack.'

She erupted into what she considered a laugh. 'Heart attack! Are
you dingbats? This old clock's good for a couple of hundred years.'
Thumping her chest, which boomed. 'All the rest's wearing out,
but the pump's as good as gold.'

She loved to fish and told me how to cook a crab without it

throwing its legs off. 'What you do, you put the live crab in the freezer two hours, then straight into boiling water.'

She killed a man once.

'I was on with this married woman and he got to hear of it and came after me in the street with a steel-tipped umbrella and before I could get the umbrella off him and throw him to buggery away from me, in the fuss it got turned back on him. When you're getting something off somebody it's a good idea to push first and then pull nice and quick. I never got to the pull. When I pushed, it went in through his temple. That part there.' And she showed me with one thick finger.

'Turned out his skull was only one millimetre thick.'

She stopped for a moment, her fierce eyes looking out across the street, mowing flat every living thing they encountered. She'd be aggressive till the instant she died. I liked that. It was a shame to think the spirit of aggressiveness weakened with the muscles, and shook with failing nerves.

'Pity,' she said. 'Never liked that woman after that. She soon took up with another male.'

Cynthia had only one tooth in her head.

'Perfect it is. The dentist says he's never seen anything like it.' I couldn't see what was so perfect about it, but it was a good tooth. Not even a filling, and all the others dropped out and the gums shrunk.

⌒

The great disappointment in her life was her two kids, two boys. They grew a bit, then stopped. Two short sons. When she sat down they were hardly taller than she was. But they made up for their lack of size: they had her heart and her energy in small bodies and fought like threshing machines.

⌒

Her father had been in the same tradition, a hard man. You didn't often hear words in praise of males in the Lover's Arms, but no one was going to risk telling Cynthia to shut up.

'He was hard, my father,' she chuckled. 'Always had it in for some bastard. Like that thieving colonel, during the Second War, at one of the ordnance depots. It took three trucks to bring back the stuff that bastard pinched from the stores. Dad dobbed him in.' She expected me to laugh with her, but I didn't find it funny.

'And at Darwin when the wharfies went on strike the old man marched 'em off the docks with fixed bayonets —'

'Alone?' I asked in all innocence.

'What're you talking about, Doc? You want me to fill this place with uppercuts? Course not on his own! Don't giss the raw prawn! Or I'll eat your pussycat for dinner.'

She was kidding, but just then Bobbie yawned, showing her needle-sharp teeth and the lovely long white incisors, as if she knew what had been said.

'Well, maybe not for dinner.' And she leaned over and patted Bobbie, one of the few game enough to do that.

'And the wharfies waited for them at the Club Hotel, but Dad's lot were lucky and still had their sidearms; they beat 'em over the head and face. Dad was having a great time, throwing 'em over the bar left and right, into the mirrors, out the doors.

'And later, coming back from Crete there was a bunch of nurses on shore, no room for 'em, and the Captain said "Cast off!" and Dad's mates all got their rifles — they were deck cargo — and they all loaded them and aimed at the Captain and said: "Pick 'em up!" and he did. They were going to leave them there without a chance. Dad's people were being evacuated, the Germans had taken the place. I tell you, Doc, there were officers on that trip marked down for sharkbait. Went over the side and no one knew a thing about it. Missing Believed Killed. MBK. In a big storm out in the Indian Ocean one of Dad's friends had one lined up at the rail, for something he'd done against the men, with a pistol in his guts and he hated that officer so much that when an extra loud clap of thunder came he fired. He was pressing it in so close the muzzle went into the wound. Had to wash the blood off the barrel.'

Sometimes they let themselves go a little when they tell me stories, Bobbie. A pistol barrel wouldn't fit into the wound its bullet made. I'm sorry to have you listening to these things. A young animal like you ought to be spared talk of fighting and quarrels, yet, I suppose, in the wild you would have to live by your teeth and claws. Of course you would. And we humans need to remember war is not separate from daily life. It's just another happening, arising from the way we live.

Poor old Cynthia wanted to say more, but Bobbie and I had to go: she was getting a wee bit ferocious. I love Australia, but sometimes Australians are hard to take.

The engineer mocks the selectivity of the lonely.
But that's not me! I've got my love.
My apartness is a cord that binds me,
As thick as the pupils of her eyes.

I stayed up late writing this, thinking of you. The night light is still on in the yellow building; the car park outside the night club — the place with the nude statues that remind me of you except that your feet are broader when you stand — is lit up with headlights as another home-going person is finished cruising for the night; the hammerhead crane on Garden Island looms bigger, it seems, than by day, side-on to me, its long end pointing east; the crews of the fire engines go for a practice up William Street, or maybe it's to accustom late traffic to the sight of them, since you rarely find in the morning that there's been a fire; the flood-lights are on in the yard where the girls wash the rental cars; the German shepherd dog takes a turn round the cyclone wire fence, just checking; a light is still on in the Park Hotel where, after work each day, the tough and travelled woman who served on ships for years leans out of her window, the tattoos on her arms visible from here; and over in the regional secondary school, on the top floor, the sisters sit up late, including the one that has a red shade on her reading light. Sometimes it feels like company just to see that red light left on late.

Just as I was putting my pen down a breath of new blossoms came riding through my window. Do you ever feel you can touch a breath of air? And perhaps hold an armful like a bundle?

How pleasant it would be to have a simple heart! And to take a gust of perfumed air as a signal, a request, part of a conversation the world is having with me.

Another warm breath from the north entered. I breathed it in deeply, welcoming its passage into my body. But when I breathed again, even more deeply, the perfume was vague, almost gone. I should have allowed it to do its gentle work alone, without trying to force it.

Conversation in Body Language

Tania Szimc was always hanging around Helen Grbevski, and when Helen was absent, Tania would just hang around. She asked questions constantly of Helen, about Helen, trying to catch up with everything Helen said, everything that was said to her, everything she did and all that was done to her. She wanted to enter into her brain, and if she couldn't control what Helen did and what Helen experienced, she would like to have known all the details, all the input. Tania had developed spinal tremor, though this may not have been a result of her nervous worries: she was a night-shelter guard, caring for derelict women, putting down fights and so on, and she'd had a number of injuries.

The trouble with Tania was that if the answers she got from Helen or about Helen were not to her liking, she would hurt herself, and things being with Helen as they are with most of us, Tania hurt herself a lot. Punching herself, hitting her head with solid household objects, jabbing pins or cheese-knives into her arms.

Helen Grbevski was a legal rights missionary to the illiterate. This was, and is, a fine thing to be: Helen, though, was held back from total commitment to it by a philosophical objection to equality, the mainspring of the drive to have everyone know their legal rights.

'Equality is a poison. The idea, I mean,' she told me. 'It's an ideal, and the people I come in contact with have come to think it's reality. Equality causes a lot of distress. People aren't equal, failure is widespread: the world should face it.'

She came to me with tit abatement. She was forty-one, Tania a hefty twenty-two.

This is the conversation I saw between them this morning. They'd dropped in at the Lover's Arms, separately, to meet; they had only one drink each. Helen was trying, by saying nothing, to avoid inflaming Tania's lust for self-punishment. (Sometimes she seemed to get enjoyment out of the effect she produced on Tania, but mostly she was a kind woman.) I settled down to watch; Bobbie watched for a moment, then lay down with her head on one arm, the other outstretched sideways.

The conversation; both standing face to face:

Tania: Twitch of the right thumb.

Helen: Laughter. Her expression gradually declining to that limp seriousness with which one observes a blade of grass.

Tania: Right foot slides a centimetre to the right rear, turning her body slightly away. Looks down. The pub carpet is swept only once a day.

Helen: Silence. Eyes held wide, like a fish rampant.

Tania: Her eyes come up to the level of a breast, linger casually, for they have seen one million two hundred thousand four hundred and ninety-one breasts (well, they *may* have! How could I possibly know?) then arrive at the chin. A scar is all that remains of a once prominent mole. Meant to be off-putting?

Helen: Determination expressed through a slight straightening of the trunk, not to be put off or put down. A part turn away, not much, not enough to mean her eyes are taken off the antagonist's general area. She can see her body, but is not favouring her with eye contact.

Tania: Her feet move, almost together, to a position in front of Helen. She does not want her to escape from greed of eyes — a message? — and need of touch and encirclement. And perhaps control. Or if not control, mutuality. Not a duel: a duet is on the programme.

Helen: Breathes out. She is satisfied Tania has not got control of her whip hand. If she continues to move, Tania will move to contain her, as she thinks; actually she will follow her. This is natural, for Tania cannot control her unless she has a massive advantage of power over her.

Tania: Her chest seems to be struggling with a need to get words out.

Helen: Her eyes catch the struggling movements, and she waits. What will be necessary to combat this new attack?

◁▷

End of body conversation; beginning of voice supplement:

'For fuck sake, guy,' Tania said, exhibiting extra body-emphasis of discomfort.

'Stop that naughty fucking,' said Helen primly, moving slightly sideways but not away, though her body maintained its east-west line and Tania had to follow her to be properly facing her, block-

ing her view, which was the price she exacted for the slightly molli-
fying gesture of not moving actually away.

From there they moved immediately together, cutting through
ritual as neatly as bolt-cutters through toes, opened the door and
went to Helen's car, parked round in the lane, where they finished
their body talk in another mode. When that was over and done
and their lusts deflated — but, more importantly, Tania's — they
drove away from the privacy of the lane, Tania sad (I could see
from the front door) and Helen beginning to come alive with
anticipation and energy, her appetite whetted by the skirmishing
and the light engagement.

> *The engineer says some women love women*
> *but most women love love.*
> *Are all our soft words together forgotten?*
> *All the aches, from the pit of the stomach*
> *to the tongue?*

It's getting very hard lately for me to walk past the cake shop
in Oxford Street, especially if I go without breakfast. (I'm really
eating well, the last few days.) Pandora's Box, they call it, unaware
of irony. They make tarts and cakes and pies and quiches in the
ovens at the back of the shop. The pleasant woman who often
serves feels the heat, and when the day's hot too, she's wiping her
full forehead and her unlined cheeks with her apron every few
minutes.

But the smell of cooking as you come near the shop! My money
seems to spring out of my purse of its own accord, demanding to
be exchanged for what Pandora describes as a Quiche Lorraine, or
a Provençal, a spinach, a bacon — I eat them all!

Or I might feel like a fruit tart — strawberries or peaches in
custard, for instance.

Sometimes, though, when I remember in time, I walk past the
shop several times, and buy nothing. That way the delight in the
foodsmells lasts longer, and my hunger prolongs the delicious
feeling of craving, and the beauty of the feeling lasts for hours.

Later, perhaps talking to Ivy or one of the Lindas, the memory
of the crusty, bacony, buttery smell of the pastry crosses my mind,
and I forget what I was saying.

I must look an idiot when that happens, but I don't mind. A good cakeshop is the soul of a shopping centre, to me.

The Hydroponics Activist

There'd been another attack on the City.

'Who is it this time?' I asked Ivy. I felt good. Early to bed and early to rise had brought its own reward: I'd missed the late movie. On the way to the Lover's Arms Bobbie and I had stopped in the street as the cathedral bells began to ring. We stood for several minutes. She appeared to enjoy them as much as I did. I was pleased with her.

'Sheena Passmore. You remember her. Used to drink here while she was going with Glenda, the bar-girl I sacked for dipping her hand in the till. The small, sneaky girl.'

Church bells are the — are the — what are they? Church bells are not lizards.

'How was it done?' I wished she'd get on with it.

'You really relish the details, don't you, Doc?' she said loudly, unnecessarily, for all the bar to hear. I waited, passing the time by imagining the incision and the amount of flap needed for a good surgical removal of her tongue.

'They cut into the side of her waist, missing the liver, and the semen was deposited in the body cavity, then the wound sewn up again.'

'A needlework specialist,' I remarked. 'Next he'll put in a zipper.'

Ivy laughed loudly. 'Jack the Zipper!' she chortled. 'Jack the Zipper! Say,' she addressed the bar, 'I've christened Old Man Death — Jack the Zipper!' She got a good reaction from the groups of women spread round the bar and the tables. Good reactions from her flock were meat and drink to Ivy's soul.

'Yes, that's better than Old Man Death. No one's been killed yet.'

One of the drinkers, an arthritic in a floral dress, said, 'Say, Doc, is there danger of poisoning from the semen? I read something about that stuff being the cause of cancer in women. Does it poison you if it gets in a cut?'

'Don't worry about it,' I said casually. 'Even shit washes off.'

The pub was alive with a common subject of conversation for some time, then a portable transistor broke that pattern of chatter and established its own pattern with a broadcast of the local Wednesday races from Canterbury.

⬯

It occurred to me that we were assuming it was the same person who made these attacks.

'Did they say how the incision was sutured?' I asked Ivy.

'Blue cotton.' That was no help. I wanted the type of suture.

Poor Sheena. She'd joined the hydroponics movement, passionately advocating soil-less vegetable-growing in the home, but, her interest wearing thin, she'd come to me convinced she had some sort of electrical brain discharge. She'd been reading alarming articles in magazines, but above all, she was a butterfly — one interest after another. I sent her to a practising physician, but I knew she'd be a prey to whatever threatening ideas she came across: you can't stop people reading. In her case it really seemed, however hard it is to admit the possibility, that only association with a male — with all the attendant frustration, disappointment, misunderstanding, utter waste of feeling and misalignment of emotions — would give her enough threatening but basically harmless things to fill her mind.

However, solutions weren't needed now.

The bar radio had seen the race won, weights right and dividends called. It was turned off. The ladies present resumed their other concerns, discussed clothes and tore the absent in pieces.

The engineer said love is just another belt in the mouth, below the belt. She said this, sitting in the shade of fig trees, sitting on collapsed and sticky figs.

What I produced and brought into the light is strong and confident, while I'm weak, abased, decayed.

Spotted Bobbie is taking a great interest in my typewriter today, standing on two legs, one paw on my desk, the other touching gently the keyboard. Her paws are too broad, she can't spread her fingers singly to touch individual keys, and this seems to frustrate her. When she touches the shiny steel control that whizzes the carriage suddenly to the left with a loud noise, she rears back a little and in the same movement aims a little blow at the offending machinery.

Just to oblige her, I put in some paper and tap away at 'Now is the time for all good men,' and 'The quick brown fox'. I do these exercises much faster than I type usually, and show off a little. She loves it, watching closely the keys flying up to hit the paper between the guides, and looking at the marks that show as the carriage moves click by click to the left.

Sometimes I feel all I need is my little place to shelter and look out the window, and my two Bobbies: one on a lead who walks everywhere with me, and the other at the end of this letter's journey.

If I could be a little closer to the second one, so far away, I would need nothing else in the world.

I never will be. I know it.

Oh, if there's a God anywhere, help me! Help me never to come to terms with this loss! Never to forgive life for what it has done to me! Never to love the sword that has pierced me!

Corkery

They called her the Skipper, she was always jumping up and down. It was nervousness, she always had a dozen things on her mind. She thought the name was a recognition — wholly unwarranted perhaps and therefore all the more precious — of her leadership qualities.

She'd come from another country to make a home for herself in the land of the dingo and the dark horse; she was a town person and feared trees.

Not that there were all that many in the City of Women — only in Hyde Park, the Domain, and specimens in the Gardens. Plus a few straggly ones battling the elements from little holes in the bitumen along one or two streets. Maybe more than a few, but not many. Corkery seemed to run into trees all the time. She'd walk on the road to get away from them.

'They're top-heavy,' she said. 'I can't see what keeps 'em upright. They say there's roots underground, but I can't see how a few roots keep 'em straight. They'll fall, I know it.'

She tried never to be on foot. She acquired a house in Liverpool Street, and a car, quicker than a lot of the girls round the Lover's Arms who'd been in the Lucky Country all their lives. And it isn't as if she didn't drink. The trees in the beer-garden of any pub she was in she kicked, poured drink on, pushed, jeered at, slapped, swore at. They were insolent trees, pious, pompous, threatening trees, with branches held out horizontally, clubs to descend on heads.

She grew her hair high, piled on top, so high she looked a hundred millimetres taller. She put a thick rubber pad in her sun hat to cushion her against the odd catastrophe. At a time when hats were out of fashion, she never forgot her sun hat. She wore it in the pub. As far as danger to her head was concerned, she had a heart as big as a half-sucked hundred-and-thousand.

⌒

One long weekend five of the girls went bush. The first day they spent at an old pub in Bega. They'd been late getting away on Thursday and got to Bega in time to go to sleep. They doubled up, two of them taking a room and letting the other three in by the window off the verandah, so they only paid for two. The other three had to clear out first thing in the morning. The two took breakfast out to them later.

Linda, the TV mechanic, was one of the five. And one of the two. She told me about it.

'This old pub had tin walls, I'll guarantee. There was this great thumping noise in the room next door, like a four-poster in labour. Whoever was in it gave it a caning. They did their de-briefing immediately and started up as soon as we put the light out. When they took a rest, probably enjoying a furburger or yodelling in the canyon, someone overhead took up the chorus. Up and down, thump thump all the time. We made a noise and banged on the walls, they took no notice. The overhead one squeaked. The pork sword hasn't lost its popularity outside our City of Women.

'I yelled. They didn't falter. When the pace speeded up and suddenly stopped, the one next door took over again. A bad night.

'At one stage I got up to go for a pee along to the communal bathroom; I met others kept awake by the love-birds.

'"Will you get on this?" they said to me as I padded up on bare feet. "The place is crawling with 'em. Talk about the muscle of spring."

'There aren't usually locks on hotel doors. I tried one quietly, the handle turned but the door didn't move. They'd wedged the handle.

'In the morning the two of us that were the official holders of the room went down to breakfast ready to grab all the food we could for the kids outside. In the dining room were other guys and girls looking round, red-eyed from not sleeping, mad as cut snakes, waiting for the lovers to come down.

'"Did you sleep?" I asked, shouldering the silence out of the way.

'"Not on your nelly," they replied. "No way. No way in the world."

'Then someone spotted one of the couples and began to give them the bizo.

'"There's one of 'em! That lot there!"

'A young guy and a girl made their way to a table, heads down. When they heard themselves pointed out, their faces got red.

'Two more came in, greeted again with a roar from a roomful of diners.

'"There's another lot!"

'They made their way to a separate table, faces red, embarrassed. Most of the girls I know would outstare Jesus Christ himself two seconds after they'd committed murder.

'"What colour's red?' I yelled.

'In the fuss and fun we got three breakfasts for the others outside, full meals. The loving pairs got up after a cup of tea.'

Linda excused herself for a minute; I went to the bar and got us two drinks.

'Down south,' she resumed, 'We camped in the bush by the sea and got ourselves settled in before we launched our boat in the surf. Out on the Pacific Corkery was green. We weren't far out; we thought she'd get over it and started putting out lines and getting into the canned beer.

'Corkery didn't get any better. With five of us jammed in a four-metre boat there wasn't all that much room to fish, but she began to supply us with burley.

'Every fifteen minutes for seven hours she was sick in the sea. She wouldn't ask to be brought in, I'll say that for her. But until we'd got a few cans down, it put us off a bit. In between gastric exercises, she lay on her back in the boat, looking up at the great blue sea in the sky.

'At least there were no trees there to worry about.

'Next day we decided to give the sea a miss and go inland to do river-fishing. We got off the Snowy Highway past Adaminaby and through Khancoban to the Murray Valley Highway. We went to a few properties on the Murray before we found one that would let us camp on the river bank.

'The farmer went through our equipment and only let us in when he found there was only one rifle between us. That was my little Rossi and it paid its way. With its help we got a big pot of Mulligan stew, enough to live on for a day or two while we got onto the freshwater fish.

'I got the ingredients, shot the animals, cleaned them and made the stew, all by myself. Some people don't like the idea of Mulligan stew. They'll eat it, but they don't want to know.

'We put the boat on the river, which had some wide spots there, like the Murray has, and fished all day for two miserable fish. Drank all the beer, too.

'The owner must have thought we were harmless, because he suggested going with us into town late in the afternoon for a beer, he in his car — which he called "the Beast" for some reason — and we went in ours. That was cool.

'We drank ourselves silly by closing time, and he wasn't any better, until we felt like going back for a sleep. But how? Outside the town there were no street-lights.

' "Follow me, girls," the farmer said, and drove out of the pub yard as if he was dying to get home.

'We followed. When we turned off the road, following his tail-light, I thought he must have taken the wrong turning. I eased up, letting him get ahead.

'We'd come through a lot of fences on the way to town, stopping to undo and tie up each gate, and I couldn't understand why we saw no gates on the way back.

' "I think he's taking us back to Sydney," I suggested.

'There were plenty of fences, but no gates. We were going too fast to make out the scenery in the headlights.

'Somehow we ended up at the homestead. We saw him stagger out of the car and make for his back door, stopping to wave. We went on down the track towards our camp. There were gates this time. We stopped to open and tie up each one.

'Next day I went up to the house to see the farmer about some pepper and hot sauce for the stew. I can't always stand the thought of what's in it, without sauce to take my mind off it.

' "Mr Small isn't here. He's out mending his fences," the woman said, pointing towards the file of fences between the house and the distant road.

' "What happened to the fences?" I said stupidly, and didn't wait for an answer. She probably thought I was stirring.

'I looked across the paddocks and worked out what happened. He's not mending fences: he's mending gates. I got the car and drove past where he was mending them. All nineteen of them were ripped open, flattened, bent. He'd come in through the lot. In the town I asked about it, discreetly as I could.

' "He goes through all nineteen every week. Mends 'em next day ready for the next weekend," they told me. "He doesn't mind who knows. With a few beers in he's not scared of anything except 'Time, gents'."

'The farmer looked and waved cheerfully as I went back past. I'd looked the other way before, I thought he might be embarrassed.

⬿

'Corkery came into her own that day. In her gear she'd brought a hand-operated generator out of her sister's PMG equipment (her sister worked on the power lines). And a pair of underwater goggles and a snorkel.

'When we got out a way from the river bank she went over the side and stayed with her head just under the surface, watching and keeping still. Her hands and the generator were just inboard of the boat. When a fish got near the long lead and the two electrodes she spun the handle like mad; the fish floated to the surface, stunned, and the rest of us, sitting in the drifting boat, scooped it up with a landing net, trying to keep as quiet as Corkery asked us.

'I'd brought several dozen cans from town. When it was dark Corkery used a torch. We knocked off catching fish late that night and since we had to clean all we caught, we were cleaning fish till seven next morning.

'Full as farts, we were. Seventy-five cod. What could we do with seventy-five cod? We stank, our fingers stank, the rims of the cans stank, but did we stop drinking?

'Not on your nelly, we didn't. Corkery was a genius. The farmer thought it was Christmas.'

⌒

'On the way back just for the fun of it, I told Corkery what was in the Mulligan stew.

' "It's baby stew. Baby rats, baby lizards, baby rabbits, baby cats, baby dogs, baby bandicoots. Baby everything." (If they'd been sheep we'd call them lambs; don't let Bobbie look at me like that.)

'The others laid it on pretty thick, too. Corkery was sick all the way back to Sydney. That girl's imagination is something.' (It is, too — you should see the way she makes up her face.)

'On the way back over the mountains we stopped off the road for a pee and found this deserted car. On the back seat was an old twenty-two, and a pile of papers tied with string. We took the rifle.'

She had finished her story. I got another drink for us.

'I thought she was known as Skipper. You never once called her Skipper.'

'Skipper's only a name they call her in the pub. I don't like to be filing bits off people when we're all out together, I like to give them respect,' Linda said. 'Until they show they're not worth it. I suppose it's what you'd call a fair go, to coin a phrase,' she said unselfconsciously. I waited for a smile, or a ghost of one, but in vain. Was she re-inventing not only male adventures, but male phrases and a male outlook? Was there some balance she was leaning towards, without being aware of it? I shivered slightly, remembering the male past, the brutal and boring past.

'Everyone's worried about things hurting them,' she added, defending her trip-mate.

'Everyone wants to live forever,' I said unthinkingly.

'Do they?' she said doubtfully, and left to do her afternoon's work. Her tool-box was blue, almost a cobalt blue except for the grey in it, and it clashed metallically as she picked it up.

I do, Bobbie. I know that. I'd live forever if I could, as long as I could get around. Maybe in sixty-two more years I'd get over the first Bobbie.

Perhaps, my dear, the lust after immortality is at heart greed. When mankind conquered the animals, after the big ones had died out, and once we'd got a code of sounds, and felt so superior to every living thing around us, we wanted more. And what is more obviously more than to live on after death?

We're such hopeless dreamers, Bobbie. Always pining after what's impossible. I've tried, during my life, always to belong absolutely to the world, to be a part of it and aware of that all the time. It's all we've got. The next thing I know I'm hoping my first Bobbie will come back or I'll see her again or even hear her name. Hopeless, aren't I?

> *I see again her cruel and merry eyes*
> *and in them a quick shadow of a child she has forgotten.*
> *My fingers follow her face.*
> *My mind clings to her.*

After lunch we'll go for a walk past the corner house where the women used to wait, in the old days, in the doorway, with an electric heater turned on and visible in the hallway to lure the poor, cold, lonely men inside for the few dollars in their pockets; past the green and yellow pub; past the house with the motor-bike parked in the tiny space enclosed by the wrought-iron fence; past the old Equity office, the coffee shop, Bill and Toni's, past Jim's and the fruit-shop; past the old 'Save the Whales' signs, 'Ban Uranium', 'Solar not Nuclear' — all the slogans we can remember, that failed to protect us; walking up hills, turning down lanes we haven't seen for months, remembering old houses where friends used to live, corners we rounded wondering what we'd see next; until my legs get tired and I broach the subject of going back home.

I *do* sleep better if I get tired at least once a day. I must remember to shut the windows against the north-easterly, which often pushes fumes from ships in.

*I'm thinking how the journey from her finger's tip to her shoulder
is such a distance, filled with territories that may never be explored.*

Winkie

Until she was brought over to meet me I'd just seen her with her
cronies, a tough-looking bunch, doing something busily with the
sports pages of the paper. She looked diligent and was concentrat-
ing: the sort of look people get when they're eating.

Winkie was always sore that her friend Stella, convicted of
abduction, carnal knowledge and rape of a male minor, had got
off with a bond, while she got two years for only carnal knowledge.
Different judges. When she was caught, the cops took her shoes
as evidence; she had to front the beak in a jacket and panties —
no trousers, no shoes. She'd gone right through her arrest and to
a cell with a belt and a scarf, since no one told her to take them
off, and she showed some pride in this; the number of young
'criminals' I've known of, especially young ones, that tried to neck
themselves once they were locked up might have made a thought-
ful prison reformer think.

Her first brush with the law was when she was caught drunk in
a car by a cop who knew her mother. This cop said, 'Give us the
keys.' Winkie gave her the keys. She felt ill. It was night and they
were near the edge of Art Gallery Road, with the water ten metres
below, and in between was a steep place thick with shrubs. The
cop threw them into the bushes and said, 'By the time you find
'em you'll have sobered up.' Wunderbar, chunderbar: it was two
hours before she felt well enough to begin looking.

The next time she met a cop she thought she was made. She
could handle cops. She and her gang of girls were in Fitzroy Park
one Saturday afternoon making a fine amount of noise, annoying
tourists, throwing things.

This cop walked up, all short sleeves and muscles and red hair and green eyes and the girls around Winkie melted away. Winkie stood her ground.

'Move on,' said the cop.

Winkie raised her eyebrows, said nothing.

'Move on,' repeated the officer. Her partner was across the street in the Croissant d'Or, negotiating the fate of two elegant cakes in the window.

'What for?' said Winkie.

Crash. Winkie hit the deck and her head didn't stop ringing for half an hour. She never answered back again.

⌒

Only once, in the time I've known her, did she open up about prison.

'Any young cock can pick on you,' she complained, 'And you have to prove you didn't touch him.'

This didn't apply, Bobbie, to the young boy she'd watched come down the street from school every day and that she finally got found with in the park at Rushcutters Bay.

'When you come out you're different. You get a job and you automatically stand over every bitch you meet. The ones that hit back or wait a bit and hit back, you settle down with. But the ones that take it, you stand over them always. You learn it inside.

'We used to have real clever girls where I was. They could make a crystal set out of a few bits and pieces they'd get from the workshop. I was with one about fifty, she could get 2UE on the grating and 2KY on the water pipe. For fire, to light up smokes, she'd get a metal button from somewhere, some cotton, and set up the button with the cotton threaded through two holes so you could make one of those whirlies.'

She demonstrated. I could see, as she did it, the prisoner with the loops of cotton, one round each hand and the button spinning in between; and the hands coming in a bit and going apart as if the cotton were like rubber, and the button spinning constantly.

'She'd spin the button on a bit of sandstone, a chip from the wall, and she'd make her fire in a matchbox with a bed of burnt cotton from a prison dress as tinder. A few of the girls had 'em. If you lit up and didn't ask if anyone wanted a light, they'd kill you.'

I asked her — I had to — if she had to be a good girl to the older women, the ones that had years to go without a male or lover.

'You know how it is with males, how in the first year of prison they find homosexuals repulsive, in the second year they start thinking a bit of bum isn't bad, and how in the third year they get nasty if they haven't got a boyfriend? Well, it's not quite the same as that in a women's prison, but a bit the same.

'While I was there a girl passed through that got into trouble all the time. We all got into trouble, but this one always whinged. She didn't realise it was always like that inside. She thought they ought to treat her nice.

'They had her do the last two years of her sentence at Silverwater and she wanted to write her experiences in prison, so she got the psychiatrist that visited her to smuggle paper in. He smuggled in toilet paper, so she wrote the stuff in a funny looking stuff I found later was called phonetic script on eight thousand pieces of toilet paper. All about the way she got belted up in the hard prison — the one that's closed now — and how the screws kicked shit out of you for nothing.'

'Did they really do this?' I asked. Sometimes I find it hard to follow what people say, especially those times I'm convinced I'm something else: a platypus perhaps, or a plump wombat.

'Listen Doc, you're in prison, you got to expect it. What do you think it is, a barbecue picnic? 'Course they kicked shit out of her. They told her to say the bruises were from falling down the steps when she went to the doctor.'

'Did she?' (I mean, people aren't in prison for being honest.)

''Course she did. Christ, Doc, wake up. Anyway, she got her story out to a publisher.'

'I've never seen it.' I feel so stupid talking to the young when they're so knowing.

'You never will. Libel laws in this country are all so tied up nothing can ever come out.'

⟫

Winkie would bite you for a drink while she still had coin in her pocket. But the thing she'd never do was say a word against the authorities, apart from prison authorities. At work she wouldn't have a bar of the union — it was a small place, making rubber fittings — the boss was the boss, and Winkie worked like a Trojan. They'd corrected her, all right.

She'd never join in the joke when one of her prison mates came in the pub to stir her and said, 'Let's get some sawn-offs and go into the bank withdrawal business.' Jail wasn't funny to Winkie.

∽

She got her name when she was a kid at school from her habit of cocking it up every chance she got and playing with it. She could make it wink at you. She could make it open its mouth and close it again and again, about as fast as a fish gulping.

She finally got it to wink at a steady boy who winked his thing back at her, got her pregnant and persuaded her to marry him. Penial servitude, one-to-life.

'Tough luck, Winkie,' the girls said. Once upon a time even marriage was a good thing, from a distance.

'So what,' Winkie said. 'Gotta get married sometime, even just to say you've had the experience. A root's a root.'

She never seemed to mind. He knocked off first where he worked, got the baby from the minders and waited with it outside the pub to intercept her before she went in, and made sure she went home with him. She was going straight.

Straight home.

Except for Saturday afternoons, when he took the baby to her parents' and his, alternately. She'd reserved Saturday afternoons for herself, a few quiet beers and a couple of bets on dumb animals. She lived outside the City and only came in to see her mates.

> The engineer insists the greatest tyrants
> Over women are women, and I agree.
> But I still won't suffer and say nothing.

There's a little Swiss jeweller in an old building in Pitt Street, and today I picked up from her a silver collar and nameplate for Bobbie. In addition to her name, there's an engraved portrait of her from the shoulders up, taken from a photograph.

I showed the whole thing to Bobbie before I put the chain round her neck. If she could only talk! It's so important to me that I hear from the person I'm talking to, whether it's a yes-or-no reaction, or something I don't even expect. But she understands, that's something.

I'm sure she understands.

In case you want something made some day, my Swiss is on the third floor in a building down towards the Quay from Park Street some little distance. What a repetition of 'some!' Do you ever find that if you look at a word long enough, although you know very well its meaning, the word itself on the page seems to become drained of meaning, even of sense? When I see 'some' again, I find it impossible to imagine there's any sense in it and no reason why those four letters should spell anything at all, or be pronounced like that. But — read it quickly, take it for granted, and the word gives no trouble, no trouble at all.

A Plateau Person

Jennifer Ezzy at twenty-three was deeply into legal and medical automation philosophy. She wasn't often at the Lover's Arms, only Fridays after five.

At all times Jennifer had a strict knowledge of what she was. But in her case 'was' meant 'had'. She counted herself as bound entirely by what she had; her own worth lay in that. What she possessed became essentially her, as a rich child feels that the possession of money is an ingredient of personality.

When she saw herself without the latest style in shoes, she was Jennifer Ezzy-without-that-style. She wanted it, she couldn't live without it, she wasn't her real self without it: she got it. She was then Jennifer Ezzy-with-that-style. Soon the shoes were part of her, no longer noticeable, having them was how she was, in herself. But she was Jennifer Ezzy without a new portable electric hair dryer. Soon she had that, too, and not long after, the possession of it was so natural to her that she might have been born with it. It had been the same with her bike, her horse, her sound system, her swimming pool when she was a child. These things were natural parts of her character: she was the sort of person who had them. Possessions grew within her, and so did Jennifer Ezzy grow within her, building up into something distant from the Jennifer Ezzy that began it. So that, viewed back along the perspective of time, there was a series of lesser Jennifer Ezzys receding back as far as the smallest one; a line of statues, all slightly different. But she wasn't free to go back and choose a compatible one to be: the Jennifer Ezzy inside impelled her onwards towards difference, constant increments of change, new levels of personality.

I wonder if when the time comes she will meet tragedy the same way, playing her demands from life by ear, listening to the necessity within; getting, rising to a new level; having, being on a level plain and seeing only the distant peaks of her desires.

Example: tragedy strikes Jennifer Ezzy. She is as she was, plus tragedy. Then loves strikes her. She is Jennifer Ezzy plus tragedy plus love. The tragedy and the love become part of her, indistinguishably.

What peaks lie before her to be scaled? Success? She achieves it. It becomes part of her. At the last, on her way up towards the last plateau, where she dies unenvied (which she could not have imagined, for she always wanted to be envied, and thought she was) she incorporates all these weighty increments, growths, personality traits. No wonder that last slope is hard to climb.

Many times, seeing her drinking there on Fridays, noticing the keen, forward-looking expression of her eyes slip and be replaced by the helpless, vulnerable look of a Jennifer Ezzy who had mortal fears, doubts even, and didn't know where they came from or how to deal with them, I wanted to go over and say something to her that would help. But what could I say? 'Oh would some power the privilege give us never to suffer the humiliation of having to see ourselves quite as foolish, ridiculous and ugly as others see us'?

No, you silly old woman. Be sensible. Don't take out your own discomforts on young people. Bobbie! Tell this crazy old woman to behave with restraint.

Or, could I say: 'Jennifer, love, don't skip any years. You're twenty-three. Don't try to be twenty-eight. And when you're fifty-eight don't try to be twenty-eight. You're Jennifer: *be* Jennifer.'

Should I say that to her? . . . Then why don't *I* do it? I, more than anyone, ought to know that just as we can rest content nowhere on earth while we have energy, so we can't rest anywhere within ourselves without that inner place becoming routine, stale and loathsome, and something to escape. And if her restlessness seemed at once grosser than the usual run, yet comic as well, wasn't it the same, essentially?

☜

What was all that about tragedy a few paragraphs back?

Ah, Bobbie, I saw it in her eyes. The recurring mortal fear she suffers from, that comes past her occasionally, trailing its rank smell, is awareness, the knowledge that comes knocking whether we receive it or not — and she is on the point of letting it in — and if we open the door and admit it, we hear a brutal voice shoulder aside the smug quietness of our minds, saying, 'Forget it! That's not how it is at all! Wrong, Wrong, Wrong!'

Final failure, Bobbie, is not another peak to climb: it's a realisation that nothing she has done or owned or been or said has made the slightest difference and she is as she started — naked and on a level with everyone else. She hasn't climbed at all. She is still standing on the featureless plain where she started, surrounded by odd objects that stubbornly insist on their own independent existence, as if all her effort had never been.

Yes, Bobbie, I know. Not only she: we too. I know it well. All of us.

The engineer taunts: you can't lose what you never had. She will always have me, though I can't have her. Cells of our bodies change, and we change, but I haven't changed.

I feel so tired today. Last night I lay awake, my head in a mess with restless thoughts tumbling over each other, clamouring for attention.

Let's get off the bitumen, Bobbie, and climb the little hill that takes us up past the parking station, and get on to the grass. It's shoes off, for me. You need no dressing or undressing, lucky thing.

We keep off the path and head towards the swings and seats and the two stone ladies. The water from the bubbler is cool if you let it run.

It's after five, but still very warm. Bobbie is hunting a cricket in the grass. She makes a little spring, coming down with her two front paws together, like hands. With her paws together like that she looks round at me, her eyes serene, almost sleepy. And begins to dab at where the cricket's sound came from, but her heart's not in it. She relaxes, sits back on her rear legs, licks at a speck of something on her chest, then settles sideways and down with a slumping movement onto her side, then stretches out — neatly, very neatly — but flat out. Eyes shut.

I haven't been able to relax like that — so immediately — since I was very young.

In the garden nearby a golden orb spider hangs in a golden web that still has two or three dewdrops clinging.

The Desalination Researcher

Lola Beach, a large over-stuffed woman I met in connection with her complaint — which had all the earmarks of urethral anguish — was found at the foot of a fire escape in Norman Street, behind Oxford. The fire escape led up to the several floors of a warehouse. She was alive; the assailant had subdued her with chloroform, had sliced into the calf of her right leg — she had wide, muscular calves, well padded — and deposited his semen there, then sewn up the site of the deposit with a short length of fine-gauge fishing line and a curved bag needle. Police arrived at this last hypothesis from the size and shape of the needle holes.

Outrage was proclaimed in the media. What danger was there of poisoning due to cell alteration that may follow a contact between semen and tissue cells? Pictures of tadpole-like sperm burrowing their heads inside the walls of rat cells harrowed that often-harrowed field, the public mind.

It seemed just another Old Man Death attack. Yet not quite the same, for a man calling himself Jack the Zipper wrote a letter of protest to four newspapers (the produce of two companies: he could have saved half the postage) complaining that this latest victim was not his work, not his style. He wanted his public name changed to Jack the Ripper, Zipper wasn't as dignified. He meant fearsome.

Lola Beach, from her bed in hospital, with her wound washed out and properly sewn with official materials, showed an interest in the public reaction to her brush with Old Man Death.

'Was he going for some kind of record?' she asked.

And 'Will I be in the *Guinness Book of Records*?'

The hospital staff, on no evidence, assured her that she would. It made her think, though. She was actually seen thinking, her mind playing round the idea of a man raping her poor old leg, a smile touching her imaginative lips, her hands wandering vaguely close to her ferocious breasts.

The real perpetrator wrote a letter, addressed, expansively, 'To the News Media', saying, 'I am privy to the essence of women. I am not a criminal, or if I am, only in part. I feel for women with the most sensitive probe known to man. You will begin to catch me, but I will proliferate; cut off another head, another will grow: there will always be more of me to come. I must immerse myself in women. I must know them.'

And a suburban headmaster, in a nearly grammatical and barely pompous letter to the newspapers, reported that the new crime had been incorporated into a group skipping game played among his nine-year-olds. It was mentioned in pop songs, obliquely referred to in new recipe suggestions on the women's pages.

Old Man Death was growing in fame, and Lola Beach was part of this. She worked at a desalination plant on the coast and when I went to visit she was full of how well the women in the ward got on together. They had in common the fact that they were victims of male attacks, and this fact had a wonderfully binding and supportive effect, and reinforced all their intimate community knowledge of subjection, and their individual histories of misery.

She advised me to cut my coat with the cloth I've got left, but after a love like ours I can love no more.

Standing with Bobbie at the top of William Street under the Coca Cola sign around sunset, the pinkening sky (is pinkening a word?) on the western horizon deepens to fire-red. And that part is three lines of a rectangle which descend from the sky, trained within two lines of buildings and hitting Park Street way after its continuation of William. The sunset red is a frame for the cunningly placed Sony sign — blue — which seems to stand on the depths of the sunset, as Harry Pearce's bullocks once walked on air, or still walk on air in those brains that provide a lodging for old memories and dead poets.

It's a sunset city. The tall buildings are silhouettes in the familiar shapes I know and love so much, and when I get an angle on the farther shore of the harbour, bits and points of light are picked out by the sun, and one by one, and often several at a time, windows catch the sun and throw a blinding reflection right into my face and I have to turn away, dazzled.

If you could *see* the beams of light! How fascinating to see those beams move gradually, as the earth moves, throwing their reflections in arcs, sliding from object to object, surface to surface, until the sun went down and the last beam disappeared.

If I could only be happy to drift with whatever current came, to float with whatever wind blows, to be an object patiently reflecting whatever sunbeams fell on me — but I can never be.

Drinking

Eva Isaacs was twenty-two when I met her; she suffered from mouth-drop and wanted me to direct her to a specialist in the new Ugandan lip-tightening process.

I met her in the Lover's Arms on a day when the dimness and the shaded lights were restful after the dazing, dazzling sun. She had never been drunk before; she was testing how it felt to drink beer. She felt she ought to share with me the feelings she detected as she kept at it.

'What line are you in?' I asked her when she sat down at my table.

'I investigate strategies whereby people ignore mass advertising,' she said, and laughed.

'I'm a failure in F minor,' she said. The laugh happened again. It started on a middling note and went immediately to a piercing high one, and from there descended in steps and stairs of sound. Getting mercifully quieter as she got down to the contralto register.

'I've never been drunk before,' she said, smiling.

'Are you intending to be?'

She lifted the beer glass to her lips. When her face was in repose the mouth sagged at the two corners. Smiling, the corners lifted. She drank, and waited, then went out to have a pissa solemnis.

'I'm heavy in the stomach,' she reported when she came back, with another unnerving laugh. 'In the stomach region. From below the ribs here, down to the pubis. My arms feel relaxed, it feels good to spread my fingers.' She drank again. Waited, reported again. I'll just set down the running report she gave me — you can get your own picture of the proceedings. I'll leave out the filling and refilling.

'My eyes feel gracious.' And I'll leave out the laugh.

'My nose is so steady. It's cooler!' Touching it.

'The side, and back side of my tongue ...' Backside of her tongue?

'The saliva seems heavy. I can feel the texture different, as between my middle tongue and down my throat. The alcohol seems to pull out the heavier saliva, but to take, itself, the middle track down.'

'I feel at ease. I feel no desire to be better dressed.'

'My upper arms are warmly cool, heavy and fattish. Why, it's the muscle, of course!'

'My toes are light and airy. Not quick, but pleased when they move.'

'I like looking at things now. Looking is gentle. Sort of benign.'

'The world is as it is, though most of it is out *there*. What is out there is not all that detailed, but easier to master than without alcohol.'

'Without alcohol, the detail and variety of the world is stimulating — to effort, and stimulating to speed of movement.' She, however, did not move.

'All of me wants to slump. It *is* slumping. My ankles, knees, bottom, waist, stomach, chest — I'm hardly breathing! Almost I get the impression that breathing is unnecessary. And my neck allows my head a freer, quieter, movement. So easy to move, so relaxed.'

'It's lovely that one is stationary. Familiar objects — some of these chairs, tables, vases of flowers, bottles on the shelf, are growing into loved objects. If I were outside now, I would be disaffected from the pursuits of the rest of the world. Being rootless, others would disturb me.'

She lapsed into silence here. Her mouth was quite down. After a space she regained her energy.

'Oh, I feel so much vigour! All of a sudden. Let's get more. Let's hurry, we must do it now!' A much larger glass occupied her for half an hour.

'If only I had a good excuse. To have more.' The words seemed to suck the breath out of her. She breathed deeply several times.

'The people. They cluster round the bar. Especially where the girl serves. They leave you to shout across all that way. My stomach feels so heavy. The rest of me is quite dead. I mean, deadened.'

She drank two more with no conversation. Instead, she seemed to travel back into her own interior. At last she spoke.

'My legs seem so unwilling. I wish you'd buck up, legs. My arms are all ... poor. My head is so slow ...'

'My legs are swirling.'

When next I saw her, she had become a convert to spirits. Now, a year later, she is a wine-jar ambulant, looking for wine.

My engineer asserts that with loving care I fashioned a rod for my own back. Is this what was happening in our moments mouth to mouth when we writhed against each other like soft and wounded snakes?

I felt a sort of lightness today, as if I could miraculously run and skip again. I didn't go that far, but the cheerfulness that welled up from within, somewhere, made me feel cheeky enough to ring doorbells, even throw things at solemn people — actually everyone I saw today seemed absurdly solemn — or to stop cars in the street and strike up conversations. (Strike up — did that come from the days of striking a light?)

Several dark deserted buildings invited me in, but I didn't want that much adventure. I contented myself with putting my hands on the tall posts carrying the high-tension electric wires, putting my ear to posts to hear the hum of forces I will go to my grave not understanding, feeling the atmosphere of a parked car and being interested that it must have come a distance to be so hot.

From the faces of people I passed, I think I must have been smiling a lot of the time. Funny how people think you're peculiar if you wear a smile.

I feel like a child again. Don't worry, it's just for a day. It's better than sitting at home, worrying myself sick about things I can't change.

At home, getting a cup out, I found a cockroach shopping around in my cupboards. I pursued it gently, caught it gently under one finger, and as gently killed it, pressing it to death.

Everything seems to uncomplicate itself, when you smile.

The Song of Georgina Washington

My mother was present on that shameful day when the first woman Governor-General, having opened the National Folk Idiom Library, was incautious enough to speak to a lone girl of perhaps eight years. That generation of children was known to be dangerous, to be approached with caution. The girl had no bag, was shivering in a light dress and wore the badge of the Broken Hill Breakaways — the alternative feminist government of that once male city. It was remembered later that she alighted from a meals-on-wheels van that paused on its rounds to the Canberra poor.

'Little girl,' said Georgina Washington, 'Why are you so far from home?' Perhaps she thought to do a good deed.

But the girl answered her in rough and grating tones, 'Mind your own business, you old cunt!'

Aides came to restrain the girl, but were told off in much the same words, except that the child very properly used the plural.

As for Georgina Washington — who had climaxed a successful legal and political career with her present eminence — she retreated. The high fur collar she wore fell off; her royal blue quasi-military jacket crumbled and tore, a small Canberra breeze playing tiredly with its two ends; her bra splintered like a tree in a storm; the semi-military trousers split asunder; her shoes shrank; the vice-regal body disappeared into the country air and all that was left was an old vulva unprotected, slipping and flapping along the street. Citizens kicked at it, as citizens will do, until someone finally picked it up and wrapped it in newspapers — both morning and evening — and left it in a gutter for eventual burial at the rubbish tip.

The little girl had disappeared inside a police van. She exhibited her tongue, but no penitence, and when asked her name said, 'Georgina Washington'.

⌒

I wish, Bobbie, you could have seen it. I wish I could have seen it. When I was small I asked for this fairy story night after night and mother obliged. And taught me the song they sang when she was young.

'Come and see the thing in the streets
Come and see how an idea withers
Royalty dehydrates in our land
Come and see people kick about
The disgusting remains of those whom
Royalty favours.
Come into the streets
Everyone in the streets
Come and bury what is disgusting
Bury what does not belong.'

I remember my mother saying she would die happy if by that time the British flag no longer flew in this country, apart from sports occasions. But when she was dying she had a premonition of a young man's boots being licked, a young man who would keep his stamp firmly on Australia's laws.

The engineer said: I feel like a block of stone, with my real shape locked inside it. I don't know my real shape.

But I know it. The breath that drives her, the spirit moving in her is the soul of the world.

I happened to look out of my window this morning as the children in the grammar school were lined up outside classroom doors, waiting to get in for their next period. One group caught my eye. Seven or eight were gathered round one girl, who lounged against the yellow brick wall. She talked a little, stopped, talked again. The rest listened.

I got out the glasses and trained them on her face. She was about fourteen, skin white as milk from the neck up except for two delicious patches of peach-bloom on her cheeks; the bones of her face, the cheekbones slanting back towards her ears, the straight nose, the clear brows, the slim jaw. Everything was harmony of the rarest kind and for two minutes I was as fascinated by her as her friends were. Her lazy eyes took them all in, from time to time, as her glance brushed lightly over them. They appeared to hold their breath, leaning slightly forward as she leaned back, their lips open, as if, knowing or unknowing, they wanted to drink that milky flesh which hid under the grey serge, and, brought into the light, would be soft and as full of sap and sunlight as fresh spring growth.

The bell rang and everywhere grey-uniformed kids were charging through green doors — they'd been newly painted in the August holidays.

☙

This is hours later. I can still feel the atmosphere outside that classroom as the others waited to feed on her every word. What could she have been saying?

Mrs Ann Grimley Enters the Cool

She was seventy-seven and came to me complaining of thumb anguish and buttock wilt. Her third career, as a limb fitter, had come to an end when she was seventy-one, after which she thought she'd like to take a rest, though she preferred not to lose her title of limb fitter. When she pronounced the words they rolled from between her lips with a satisfaction that might have derived from their medical and technical overtones.

Her second career had been in meat, she worked in abattoirs up and down the state; she'd been on a slaughter line for eighteen months, before the automated line and the gas stunning process.

In the butchers' shops in Oxford Street she was often both a problem and an enlightenment to staff and clients.

'We used to throw tails away!' she would beef out as some citizen was contracting to buy cheap meat. The citizen would often shrink a little to escape attention. Even though widespread poverty had been around so long that it seemed endemic, sufferers from it were still embarrassed.

Her first career had been as wife and mother. This she rarely mentioned.

When she came to me and I'd sat her down and so forth, her first words were a question. 'Is it true you can only love something for which you have a certain contempt?'

'If that's how you're made — yes!' I said. Not really off balance, I like to think. Seventy-seven? Yes, if that's necessary for you.' Who could it be? Love at seventy-seven? I said to myself. Don't laugh, you!

But contempt at that age; who'd bother? Laughter bubbled up in me. Not at her; I don't know what it was directed at, something in me had to laugh. She took it well.

She wanted me to discuss it further, or — worse — tell her what she should think, but I wasn't equal to it. Was she worried about her past family, which she'd abandoned to have a more interesting life? It seemed not. After a few sentences to and fro, it turned out to be her dog, Fazackerly, that she loved. Though among her other experiences her time on the meat line was replete with memories of the warmest kind.

'As a member of the canine race Fazackerly had never really got used to us. I always took him to be a representative of the doggie race; I only knew dogs because I knew him. His civilisation had broken up long ago and he was one of a remnant, a sad and sorrowing remnant that let their bodies yield up their procreative power to the humans' knife. If they'd got together and mapped out a program, it may well have been within their power to butcher all humans in their cots in the first year of life. Only their goodness stopped them from this act. I've seen Fazackerly wistfully watching dog games and sporting meetings; I've seen him thinking "What we might have been if we'd stayed together in packs. They split us up; we allowed their easy scraps to tame us, we turned our backs on effort and danger, loneliness and hunger and cold. We are slaves, worth no more than plants to be culled. Weeds in animal form. Self-reliance counts for nothing now, there's a dog-catcher at the end of every street if you are masterless." '

'Where's Fazackerly now?' I asked. Perhaps he was waiting outside. We could have him in, to think some more. Aloud, for preference.

'Ill,' she replied dolefully. 'He's had the usual doggy ailments; I've wormed him regularly, he's had hormone treatments for his moods and his personality difficulties; he's been sick with colds, afflicted with pneumonia, tortured by intestinal disorders, and come through them all, thanks to modern doctors.'

'And drugs,' I added, to be helpful. Bobbie lay flat out on the carpet, not paying much attention. That morning we had gone for a walk along Art Gallery Road and Bobbie captivated some children by springing up on to the back of the first bronze horse, the one just this side of the Gallery steps. She looked cheeky and comical sitting behind the horseman, and after a bit moved carefully round and sat over the shoulder of the horse. I was proud of her, and of the regal way she looked round.

'And drugs,' repeated Mrs Ann Grimley dutifully. 'But there are no doggy drugs yet for cancer.'

'Poor little thing. Where?' So that was her real reason for coming.

'The throat. And spreading into the jaw.'

And similar harrowing things. When Fazackerly died Ann Grimley took to coming to the Lover's Arms once or twice a week, then settled into a steady routine of coming each afternoon around four, leaving at six. Then she stopped coming. I've pieced the rest together from fragments possessed by other women and passed to me bit by bit.

⌒

Mrs Grimley carried her afternoons round with her under her brown overcoat. They were always hot, still, torrid, even drenching. She sweated a lot at night, too, as well as by day, and at a certain stage of the afternoon, often just after lunch, Mrs Grimley would take out a razor blade from a dark brown and still-shiny leather wallet, and draw it gently down that part of the afternoon that hung stifling in front of her. It would part slowly, and with a swish! Mrs Grimley would enter the cool.

One Tuesday in February, she took a weapon not from her wallet but from a pocket. It was a long curving thing, browned from use and exposure, probably due to the natural oils of her hands, and slashed it down the gentle flesh-coloured folds of that particularly hot afternoon.

It came apart quickly, as you would expect from the sharpness of a hollow-ground German steel cut-throat razor, but the rest of the afternoon collapsed and fell in on her as well and they took her away and cleaned up.

⌒

Every time I think of her now I remember what she asked about feeling a certain contempt for something you love, and I wish I'd asked her what she had in mind. Did she mean the shattered relationship with her family, or her working life, or the dog Fazackerly? If it was Fazackerly, did it mean she could love the dog better and manage the relationship, including all the understanding and forgiveness the animal needed, if she felt she was the responsible one in the relationship and therefore in certain respects superior to Fazackerly? Or was the implied superiority no more than knowledge of him and his needs, no more than understanding?

I should have asked more questions. The most important feelings often are those left hanging at the end of an unfinished sentence — in this case a question not followed up — and it was my fault I knew no more. I wish I had a Did for every Should.

The engineer tells me the secret waits for the flash of insight that comes to eyes unclouded by filaments of ambition, greed, longing. I need no secret, only an answer: what did I do with time before you came?

The school holidays are here again. Perhaps the beautiful girl who got so much attention was talking of where she was going for the break.

The yard is silent. As usual someone has left the period bells connected; every forty minutes they ring out and nothing moves. After three or four days they will be switched off.

Several cleaners tidy up the yard; painters have brought their vans in and are putting scaffolding together. A pile of sand in the top yard stands there waiting, and husky girls are unloading bricks.

I miss the noise of the children, their turbulent exit from classrooms, the headlong hurry of latecomers with bags flying, faces flushed, hair all over the place.

I miss the games of handball played on the little area set aside for seniors outside the art room at the top of the main school.

I miss watching the little groups in the lower playground as kids join and leave them, some unhappy spirits wandering back and forth from group to group, others forming the stable core of one group.

Most of all I miss the shouts and laughs and the constant movement.

(I will never be satisfied with being relegated, rejected: I will never admit it's all over. I will *not* go quietly.)

Mouse

They called her Mouse because although she was quiet as a mouse on the football field, she never finished a game without a black eye. She'd go into rucks regardless — headfirst, boots and all. It didn't matter whose side you were on, if you were on the ground anywhere near that ball she'd tread on you, kick you out of the way, it didn't matter.

She'd stayed single long after most of her friends and teammates got some backward male clown into trouble and got married. She worked in the metropolitan abattoirs. Her most spectacular mistake, when she'd been there only two years, apart from several upsets with the gut bucket, was to let out the pigs.

There were only nine, but they escaped into scrub and bred in a swamp. Organised shoots couldn't get all the escapees, so they got hunters in and built pits to catch the suckers and put them back into the process, and finally shot or captured the rest. Mouse didn't go on any of the shoots, she couldn't bear the thought of shooting down living creatures.

She worked in the gut section most of the time. She'd had her stint of killing, but got sick of it. The other killers had to be rested after a bit. It got to them. Mouse went back a second time on to the line, then was rested again. She never went back to it.

To bleed them properly, you couldn't kill them outright. You had to half kill them — cut their throats and let them gush blood and die at the same time. If you killed them instantly you didn't drain all the blood. The screams never went out of your head, she said.

Somehow, though she was one of the most harmless girls you'd ever meet — she was twenty-eight then — she seemed to get pushed into trouble.

At the Leagues Club at the Junction one Friday night she bumped a dart player's elbow. The woman pushed her, she pushed back. One of those confrontations where you sway back and forth and nothing much happens. Two of the other's friends came over and broke it up before it developed.

She thought nothing more of it until in the car park she looked up from unlocking her car door to find five large girls waiting for her. She got a kicking in true Australian sporting spirit. It wasn't a really bad kicking, three of them had soft shoes. After a really bad kicking you're not right for six months, and not really right then.

She took to going out with a red-haired girl after the redhead suggested it. This one went with a lot of others, but Mouse didn't mind, it was the usual thing.

They got thicker and thicker, and when Mouse was with anyone, it was the red-haired girl. They began to talk of getting married, to be together forever. The red-haired one knew where they could get a baby and knew of a place they could live and painted pretty word pictures of house and garden and parenthood and things seemed to be getting settled without much effort on Mouse's part. She began to build her future on the prospect.

Once when they had a ding-dong row during which Mouse told her to go to hell and stay there forever — just temper and not all that serious — Celia turned up next morning at the abattoirs with police and pointed to Mouse, 'That's her.'

The cops invited her into the car and Celia said, 'You promised.' Celia was threatening to get Mouse on breach of promise.

One of the cops said, 'You have to prove you didn't.'

The upshot was, Mouse married her, which was what Celia

wanted. For the next months Mouse had it constantly on her mind that she was going to be a parent — half a mother to a nice little kid. But it wasn't to be. She came in the Lover's Arms one day and said, 'The arrangement's fallen through. No kid. I've got married for nothing.'

'Bad luck,' everyone said. Celia had tricked her and gone back on everything she said about a child. She just did it for kicks. But some of the girls round about got worse deals than this. Mouse soon forgot her troubles. Most of the girls had to get married or wanted to know what it felt like, and it didn't matter all that much who they were late home to, the more home-loving partner carried on the same.

The only difference her married state made that I could see was that when you told her something she looked at you a lot longer than she used to, and she liked you to repeat it before she believed you.

◂▸

Mouse would get steamed up over little things, then subside quickly. There had been trouble at work and in the pub later she tongue-lashed the absent union advocate. A few minutes later I mentioned the advocate and she wondered what I was talking about.

But she was capable of more passion than we knew. One day she found Celia had gone outside the City and had been with seven truckies. Not perfectly good girl truckies: enemy truckies. That's all we knew. Not where, not when. Someone just said, 'Mouse found her missus with seven truckies yesterday. Males.'

That night around six on a Thursday when the pub was alive and pretty loud and the beer and wine and spirits swilling everywhere and the girls all edgy for conflict and eager for the weekend with purses full of pay, in walks Mouse.

Mouse is pretty tall, you'd notice her any time. But this time you notice her sooner. Her movements are quick and jerky, and her face white. There's blood on her shirt; not much, just enough to be seen all over the pub that it's blood. Out of sight you can see she's carrying a royal blue plastic bag. You can see the top of it.

A lot of us stopped what we were doing and watched her. Even Bobbie seemed to sense something — probably the tenseness in us. She didn't look round the bar as she usually did, and recognise us one by one. Just looked straight ahead.

'Two beers,' she said to the bar girl, a casual who'd only been there a week and was due to cop the sack for tickling the peter. Ivy was right onto her; there was even a stranger in a mid-grey suit and blouse at the bar watching every time she rang up a sale.

The girl pulls two beers. One's got a collar that's too deep altogether.

'Fill it up,' Mouse says. No please, no nothing.

She fills it up, hands it to Mouse all slopping with froth.

By this time half the bar's watching. You can actually hear what Mouse is saying.

'One for me,' she says, and moves the second beer to the left of her.

Mouse reaches into the plastic bag and brings out a woman's head by the hair and sets it on the bar facing the beer. The lip of the glass is on a level with the head's eyes. It's the red-headed girl that trapped Mouse when she thought marrying was necessary for the kid's sake. The eyes are not closed, quite. An innocence, charming and unexpected, possesses the bloodless face, radiating from those quiet eyelids.

The entire pub stopped. Even the pool game. I can feel that silence even now.

'Drink up, you fuckin' bitch,' Mouse said in a loud voice, dropped the plastic bag beside the head, left the head there and brought her beer over to us to have a mag before the cops came. She knew someone would sneak out and ring them.

'You heard about her,' she said. It wasn't a question.

We heard.

'I burned the rest up the backyard in the barbecue grate,' she said.

They gave her life.

❧

Others in circumstances they couldn't wear took their own lives. But getting put inside for life isn't too bright, either. The bar doesn't open at ten every morning in jail.

❧

She went funny in stir. I visited her several times and all she'd talk about was a mouse. A real mouse.

This little prisoned animal came out when she wasn't looking and Mouse left bits of food for it, trying to make friends. She didn't

131

team up with any of the humans there; she was respected for her record, but avoided.

'They don't let you keep pets here. They'll spray her if I let on. But I wish she'd realise I don't mean her any harm.' Like in the armed forces, anything from a spider in your tent or cabin, to a cockroach or a rat was a pet.

Mouse tried everything she knew, but the mouse would not be tamed. All it would do was come to the entrance of its hole and look steadily at Mouse with bright, unblinking eyes. It was a personal defeat; she became more and more morose.

Finally she hanged herself in her cell. They say it takes up to fifteen minutes to die by strangulation when you're hanged. The makeshift rope she'd hanged herself with must have lasted only a few minutes more than that before it broke. One of the girls — in for armed robbery and attempted murder — told me that when they found her there was a mouse sitting up on her face. Looking right at home.

I wish Mouse could have known.

Poor Mouse. Hell is not other people, Bobbie. Loneliness is hell.

> *My engineer says I have wounded her with a special wound,*
> *and only strangers can heal her.*
> *Time has wounded me,*
> *wrinkles and trenches have made my face a stranger.*
> *Youth! I've forgotten its name.*
> *And she says she's wounded.*

Last time there was a carnival in William Street, the traffic was stopped and a solid mass of people packed the roadway and footpaths right up to King's Cross. Usually I like those occasions, but not that time. There was something about the faces that I'd never noticed before.

A violence; an unseeing, unregarding stare; an obtuse carelessness of others; a blind, shallow connection with all the rest; an ugly comfort at being surrounded by beings so like themselves. They idled, hurried, kicked cans and discarded food, sat in gutters; everywhere they went they seemed to be seeing nothing and no one, and when there was finally no one to see, only others like themselves looking for something to look at, they showed no disappointment. It was as if they had never expected anything.

And the coarse children!

And the babies with brutal faces!

I hate disliking people. In such moments I think of birds, which move in the air like fish in the sea; each falls to the bottom when dead, each has a freedom we ground animals don't have.

I wonder where I really belong? It can't be this world: it's no sort of home to me. The place where my roots are, and to which I am tied, is a person: it is where she is.

❧

When I got home I stood for a long time with my head and shoulders out of the window in full moonlight.

Big Jill

Her eyes had a sad expression which was permanent. Her ambition, her entire purpose in life, was to lose weight: that's what they told me about her. But she had deeper thoughts. I found out.

When I first set eyes on her I noticed three funny lumps of flesh sticking out from her neck where her collar opened; it was a day when she came to the Lover's Arms fresh from a day of contretemps, accident and general mess. She worked in the naval yards. She'd been checking a new boiler in a destroyer, and a woman has to do her soot-blowing, hasn't she?

'How was I to know they were painting the ship? Fourteen on deck splashing white paint around and you'd think someone would tell the poor boiler operator. We'd just had a new boiler drum fitted and had been giving the boiler a test. You have to soot-blow a boiler, there's no getting away from that. How can I help which way the soot blows?

'Away I go, doing my job, and inside a minute there's yells and curses coming down the pipe. The soot's blown from the tubes and instead of taking it up high or away over the suburbs, the stupid wind's taken it down all over their white paint. So it's a mistake. It isn't as if they had to pay for the paint. No one pays for the paint, only the Gov'ment. And it isn't as if they'd be having a holiday when they finish the job. But no, they have to put the dirty on me. Some smartarse, just because I put soot over deck and paint and crew, she gets a pan of soot and puts it down the fan intake, my fan for fresh air. All over me. Black as the ace of spades.'

She was sadder still come Anzac Day, the one day of the year they let men into the City. I'd never been to see a march, and just looking at pictures on a screen or on a lump of paper doesn't affect you. Yet Big Jill wiped a tear from her eye when the pub TV showed the second Ninth swinging round Pitt Street into Martin Place, and one of the bands had three little kids on bagpipes, no more than eight years of age. I'd had no idea any of that could be real, no idea Big Jill's remembrance was a real emotion. I'd always thought of it as a dead memory.

The whole pub thought she was a bastard. Not a bitch: a bastard; bitch was too weak a word. She had only one kid left at home, the others had all left — they couldn't stand her — and this kid was eight, smoked cigarettes and things, and wouldn't go to school unless the teacher called to pick her up.

Big Jill was capable of coming out with pearls of wisdom such as that all men ought to be savagely punished in this way or that, the latest being sweeping the streets with toothbrushes. I don't know if the others will remember, Bobbie, but wasn't that one of the ingenious self-esteem-reducing ploys used against Jews in Europe all those years ago? Males as the world's Jew?

◠

On that Anzac Day I found what made Big Jill tick.

Her father was some sort of war hero — he went round killing lots of people — and it made a difference to her. He had a string of medals and lots of stories and Jill always wanted to be like him. A hero. She'd done karate for years, but all it had given her was trouble with her tendons and an arthritic condition in her knees and finger joints. Her surface blood vessels seemed to burst easily. She was helpless. Every time she had a blue with one of the tougher women on a Saturday afternoon, she got done. Done like a dinner. She was made of different stuff from her dad.

Another thing. Big Jill *was* a bastard, a real bastard. Her old man wasn't her real old man. She was trying to live up to an idea of someone else's father. It was all she had. And she used to sneer to see others' faults mirror her own.

◅▻

Some time later she came in looking rather nice and telling me, and others, all in strictest confidence, of course, of her widower. One of these animals, outside the City, had taken a fancy to her. She was thirty-nine and he sixty.

'Every time I go there I cop a new dress or jewellery, sometimes things I don't want and I change 'em with people here in the pub for things I want. He's made of money. Never spend it all in the time he's got left. Just made another investment of eight hundred thousand and that was just proceeds from other investments. Christ knows how much more he's got. He waits tea till I get there and starts cooking when I arrive. What do I do? I lob, lie down on the lounge, say I'm tired, and he's looking after me, slippers and all, house-gown, lovely food. Eating out of my hand.'

She kept that up for months. She also sprouted more lumps.

They came up under her ears, on the back of her neck, right up under her chin and down her throat and chest. You could see them when her shirt was open, between her breasts, and even mounting the slight rise towards those same glands.

Last of all, they began to appear on the sides of her face. They weren't round lumps, they stuck out like horizontal peaks of rock except they were flesh-coloured and soft, just like the surrounding skin. Stuck straight out. Her widower still loved her, she said he said. But she took to buttoning her shirt.

'He loves me,' she joked. 'Lumps and all.'

Women looked at their drink glasses just in case, hoping they didn't get one she'd drunk out of. I couldn't help feeling sickened at the sight of her. She looked like one large irregular cancer in human shape.

'Does he still kiss you?' asked Ivy.

'Sure he does. Between the lumps,' said Big Jill, her sad face gathering into an alarming smile.

It may have been true. However, one night he put the bed light on and found his tongue had been playing hopscotch on a patch of soft, jutting lumps.

He showed her the door naked, threw her clothes out after her and didn't even say goodbye. She dressed sadly in the front garden and walked towards home. She walked so slowly and so sadly that

135

a patrol car stopped near her and invited her to come for a ride. She was too sad to say anything in her defence to the two officers, one of whom was a girl she recognised from the karate school. In the cell she stood miserably near the door — while the drunks and quarrelsome old ladies bickered and shouted near their pallets — until they let her out, undrunk and a dollar lighter.

'I often think of myself, these days, as not being entirely present,' she said morosely to me the next day. 'And I think of myself as "she".'

'The third person,' I supplied.

'No, just two,' she said patiently. 'I think of myself as another person. Two altogether.'

~

She arranged to have her own glass in the pub and drink out of it all the time, just so the other ladies wouldn't get the shits at drinking with her. She couldn't even be in a shout, the glasses might get mixed. I was going to buy her a patterned one, but maybe that would be too much.

And she took to spitting, as if there was something nasty in her mouth and by enough spitting it would come out. It didn't. It was always there. She was that thing. They began to call her Hot Plate, because she was always spitting.

She was really sad now, sad all the time. I should have guessed what might happen. But why kid myself? What could I have done? What would I have done?

~

A new section of roadway in the City was being closed off to traffic by some politician, opening it to walking citizens. They called the politician a 'dignitary' just as they did in the past. Some honours and perks are too tasty to change.

Big Jill was full of it. This was fame, this was headlines. And so close, only three streets away.

'Every thing they do gets on the front page of the papers,' she marvelled. 'No matter what they say. And on television.'

She hungered for a headline — just one, just once — as some hunger for security and pensions, even pensions in the afterlife in some calm, beautiful, entirely imaginary place.

'I'll go to this,' she said. 'It's this afternoon. See how they handle their publicity.' And she laughed, for once. It was a type of bursting, an uncontrolled explosion, that laugh. Not a pretty sound. 'Just in case I'm famous one day.'

Just for good measure, to demonstrate her high spirits, she let go with one of her ideas against males. The rest of us were happy enough to let the subject die, but not Hot Plate, spitting down near the cigarette butts.

'Blind a male a month,' she pronounced. 'To make up for the monthly torture we went through before the City was cleared. A pocket, battery-operated laser. Straight in their eyes, one eye at a time. All these one-eyed males going about, easy to pick off the second time, then they're blind. Great idea?'

'Just *great*,' I heard myself say, but Jill didn't register tones of voice.

◠

We heard about it in the Lover's Arms that night. The papers said: 'Woman Kisses Politician', 'Kiss of Death', 'Omen for Road Toll', 'Bad Luck for Shops'. Hot Plate had worked herself up to the front of the crowd just as the politician was about to cut the ribbon opening the street to shoppers and pedestrians. She spat, looked to see if the cameras were aimed, then ducked under the arms of the crowd-stoppers and ran over and planted a loud kiss on the face of the dignitary, who reared back as if in fear of her life. A nervous young cop, just out of police college and with her hair in a rather attractive page-boy cut, alert for trouble from the rabble, drew her pistol and shot Big Jill dead as a maggot.

Dead, she was news. TV cameras were on her, got the whole thing; lumps, bullethole appearing in slow motion with the entry of the bullet, the stagger, the fall, the crash to the bitumen, the bounce, the awkward looseness, the stillness, and for a day Big Jill was famous.

The ladies in the Lover's Arms shook their heads. It was no kind of boost for a respectable pub.

◠

She was a mess, Bobbie, wasn't she? It's usually only males that go about in fear that they're not man enough. Women are usually horrified that people will think they're only women.

The engineer finds the agonies of the world are her agonies; she can hide from them no longer. Therefore she's gone to find and face them. Each morning I wake and know the world and its agonies are trivial beside the ache of suddenly missing her. It happens every day and not getting less. And when I go to bed, too, with all that room under the sheets, alone.

I was still thinking of poor Jill this afternoon as a great blast of sound rushed in at my window. Over at Garden Island a fierce column of steam pushed up into the tall air from one of a mass of funnels. From here the navy ships are a tangle of shapes. I saw, then, a fat navy helicopter bellying forward, guarding the rear of a big grey ship with a number 21 near the front; this ship was nosing slowly among the tangle, ready to berth.

I watched while this happened, until all movement had stopped. A flag was run up, with red and white vertical stripes. The helicopter was up and away, having a trip round the harbour. I sat for a long time, thinking of what the crew would see on such a trip, and made myself quite envious. Bobbie lay stretched on her rug, sleeping.

Two women fished from the end of Number 8 wharf. They didn't care that the sun was blazing down on the water. It was going to be a night of ships and stars and twinkling shore-lights.

◯

The wind over the city has held its breath all day.

When I sit and think, I know that if I were rational down to my toenails I'd accept that whatever happiness I'm ever going to get, I've got.

I'll never accept that. Never.

The weight of life and its curses and all eternity press on those who take meekly what life hands out; who forgive others when they should strike back; and on those who are weeping now, for they'll weep forever and the world laugh.

Jack the Zipper Strikes for the Heart

Old Man Death's latest victim was Maggie Catchpole, whose only worry until the fatal day had been ankle mould and a fear of clitoral combustion. She always sounded to me as if she would have welcomed sickness, to have a reason for the ache inside. She had started off after university in work desensitisation, transferred to chess therapy and had become a specialist.

One who signed a letter to the newspapers as 'Not Gay Anymore' had watched the cutting of Maggie Catchpole. The onlooker had not reacted well to her close view of bestiality, even though for years, she said, she had watched similar acts on film, and since childhood had avidly read such things in books and arousing magazines such as *Wound, Slit, Hack.* She said she was still in a state of hysteria, alternately laughing and weeping, never silent. One sex does, another suffers.

Her story of what she saw was confirmed by the condition of the body. In broad daylight the male assailant had slipped into the City by night and hidden in a storeroom in the basement of a block of apartments.

He made his way up the fire stairs and entered Maggie's bachelor apartment on the western side of the building. The letter-writer was in a place that overlooked Maggie's room and had used binoculars. One sex looks, another operates.

Maggie's chest had been opened — the anaesthetic was not mentioned — and the ribs clamped back. The heart was pulled forward and the rapist used a sharp vegetable knife — Maggie's vegetable knife — to make an incision at the lowest, rounded point of the heart. This had of course killed her, but that seemed to be not the rapist's main concern. The voyeur reported that the rapist's organ was out and ready and as soon as the incision was made, thrust into the heart.

Perhaps a criminal, a murderer, is one who follows desires as freely as a small child does.

The raping movements continued for some minutes, then ceased. The attacker didn't bother sewing her up, just left her dead, ribs still clamped open, vegetable knife stuck at a jaunty angle in the left lung.

The unknown viewer continued her letter: 'Once man made

God, a Devil was necessary. Now God is dead, or dying, when will the Devil go away? Or is the Devil the immortal?

The engineer asked: must the thing that kills me pass through you first? — on a day when she tried on her new white dress with the red hem?

I have never seen a roomful of flowers, but I have seen her in her white dress.

On the night Bobbie the Second came to me I felt so hollow, so dry inside in places where I should be overflowing. An ache of emptiness, under my ribs, was exactly her shape.

Bobbie's scratch on the door could have been a burglar or break-in, but I opened not caring what it was. She stood there, looking up at me, making no move.

'Come in,' I said, as if she were human.

She looked past me, up at my face again, and slowly walked in. She was in excellent condition, eyes bright, nose glossy and moist, fur clean.

She stood in the middle of the room, looking about, taking in everything, then back at me as I closed the door.

'And who might you belong to?' I asked. As if anyone could belong to anyone else.

She continued to look at me. I remembered my manners. There was a nice rug she could have.

'If you want to stay, we can make this yours,' I told her.

She must have been tired, for as soon as I spread the rug she lay down gratefully and went to sleep. I watched her, a little nervous sometimes, and when her eyes moved under her eyelids I wondered what dreams she had.

I fell asleep in my lounge chair and woke, alive, in the morning. She was on two legs looking out of the window. I was so happy to have her to talk to, I called her Bobbie.

From that day I've never bothered about why she chose me: it doesn't matter. It's so good having her, and having someone to say Bobbie to.

Slaughter in the Pets' Home

There is no more to love than its actions, some say.

When I walked down to the bottom of Forbes Street to Suzanne Koch's veterinary establishment, there she was on the pavement delivering a lady dog of pups. An anxious owner had brought them, but the expectant mother couldn't wait to get inside the clinic. Suzanne worked fast and the mother dog efficiently, and in no time three babies were out and two to come. The mother dog licked off their cauls as if this was an everyday job, as indeed it was.

'Do you get many animals picked up off the streets?' I asked.

'Thousands. I don't know why, but being on the streets is demoralising to both people and animals. Thank What or Whom I don't deal in humans. Maybe it's the sight of shelter and homes all round, with only the outside walls to be seen and all that light and warmth way inside, unreachable. I pick 'em off the streets, or the council women bring 'em in and they can be claimed in fourteen days. A percentage are put to sleep right away.'

She carried on working, supervising a mother who needed little supervision. 'Put to sleep, did I say? I kill 'em, snuff 'em out. Then every morning, that's the killer, every morning it happens to be the fifteenth day for some of the poor bastards, and unclaimed. It's like being commandant of a death camp. The choice of which ones every morning is the agony of it, and once I've made up my mind I go ahead and do the job; but that head-down, going-straight-ahead, doing-the-job is the worst thing of all, because it's the job part of it that gives me what good conscience I have, and this job shouldn't. It's as if, because everyone with a job has to do it, I stand back and leave responsibility with the job. But the job is only a word. Jobs can't feel, jobs can't be tried for murder and cruelty and following orders at some pets' Nuremberg ...

'Then I play Handel's Largo on the sound system in memory of the poor devils I've just stuck a needle into. Sometimes I find I've turned it up too loud, to drown my thoughts. It's a jail for animals, that's what it is, it's not even a knacker's — no one eats them, no one benefits. Maybe if the hungry ate cats and dogs I wouldn't feel so bad about it. Or even if hungry cats and dogs ate 'em.'

It was really getting her down.

'If it gets on your works like this, so that you moan all the time, why don't you leave?'

'I can't just up and leave! I'm unqualified for anything else. Killing is my bag, and keeping order, organising so everything is peaceful no matter what has to be done.' And she looked so sure, yet so near to tears, that I couldn't say another thing.

'If I leave, there's hordes of uneducated kids straight out of school willing to take it on, machine-made kids, with no more idea of mercy than a plastic Virgin and Child.' Which stood on a mantel over the dummy fireplace.

An assistant came out with equipment to clean up, and take the wriggling newly born inside. The mess and bits of caul and slime and blood was indeed all over the place like a mad male's shit.

I'd seen Suzanne Koch before, for stomach wilt; she was forty-three, a fine age for it. She had no complaints now but wanted me to see her chief supervisor, courtesy title for a middle-aged woman whose family had grown and gone, who had gratefully re-entered the workforce and now had some authority over the juniors who cleaned and swept, prepared needles and looked after the burners, the holding cages and food issue. This lady was dying and had a horror of being in hospital. She'd been discharged to die at home, but didn't like it there either; Suzanne allowed her to use the spare room in her quarters on the premises.

She was wasted, having begun to refuse her food — you know the stages — and not far from coma.

'Is she eating?' I said to Suzanne quietly. I had to say something, the woman was watching me.

'She won't, naughty girl.'

That appeared to be that. We stood over her, heads bent, watching her watching us. Her fingers stroked the sheet below her chin in an investigative, almost a critical way.

She moved. She wanted to speak. We went closer to this object and bent down to listen.

'I . . .' and she paused for breath to say the words she had no doubt prepared in case someone came by.

'I . . . will get it . . . won't I?'

'Get what, Emma?'

'The . . . promotion? . . . Won't I?' Her breathing was depressed, she had to concentrate her strength to space the words evenly.

'For years she's wanted to be considered for promotion to manager of one of the smaller pets homes in the suburbs,' Suzanne whispered to me. 'It's the next step up the ladder.'

'Your application is in, darling,' she said. 'That's all I . . .'

'Yes, I've seen it,' I interrupted. 'I'm from the Department.' Lying was a small gift to a dying human.

'And . . .?'

'Application approved!' I said loudly and cheerfully. Suzanne can have had no idea of the ferment of ambition within her helper.

Emma relaxed and smiled over parts of her face. The skin was nearly transparent.

'I'll be a manager,' she breathed, more quickly but very softly.

'You *are* a manager,' I said. Suzanne looked at me, I shook my head to wave her look away. This was no time for cruel truth. Death needs mercy more.

'A . . . manager,' she smiled with the angelic last smile of the nearly dead.

We stood, smiling. At least I hope Suzanne was. I was. I wasn't game to look sideways.

'A manager.' She said it again. The taste of the word was delicious, full-bodied, nourishing, the sum of Emma's human desires.

'A manager.'

⌒

She lapsed into a coma that afternoon, still beatific. It's blindness and amnesia, Bobbie, to find anything novel or special in present-day patterns of behaviour.

If there is no more to love than its actions, then perhaps there is no more to its actions than the sum of human feeling.

I don't know if I've got that round about. I'm writing this at night and the memory of the mother dog and the fifteenth day and the furnace and Handel's Largo and poor Emma and her hunger for promotion up to her last breath, all together do something not quite usual to my eyes, and it stops me from thinking absolutely clearly. On the other hand it may be the wine, a '74 Padthaway red I've had for years.

⌒

We went walking before dawn today. The street-lights were on and only a few people about. For a change we walked the narrow lanes. Dogs barked from behind their safe fences. We crossed William and went down the paths of Woolloomooloo, past the

Atlanta, past the Cathedral Hotel. Dark was clamped down like a lid on the city; brave electric lights in spots and patches tried to resist.

The first glimmering of dawn came when we were passing the wharves in the bay. The gold of Centrepoint's tower caught the first light, while around us the houses were dark and asleep. There's something secret about being up and about when everyone else is unconscious and helpless, something powerful. I can understand that being a burglar would be a special feeling.

Dawn behind the neons came with watery green and a pink-gold mist. I began to yawn. Bobbie looked up at my open mouth and headed immediately back home.

It's strange sometimes to feel thoughts are being thought *for* me. As when we used to have our talks, you and I, and find we were thinking the same thing. Finding the same things funny.

Now my thoughts, like little waves, little weak waves, break on the shifting shore of the world as it is. The thing I have lost — snatched cruelly away — was never more mine than when it was gone.

Janey the Jailer

She was descended from a Yankee who came south to Huntsville in eighteen eighty-one. My record of conversation doesn't say whether she meant Huntsville, Alabama, or Texas — not to mention Missouri, or Tennessee. She was sixty-four and came to Australia to retire. No family, just to die.

And to get away. But she brought it all with her. Her life, her past, it was all inside her, fighting to get out.

For forty years she'd been a warder in the prison in her home town and for the last twenty on death row.

'They reckoned I had a better touch than most. I didn't act

scared, or speak rough to 'em. You see, Doc, when I was there the states had been waiting for a ruling from the Court for years. A lot of the girls on death row had been there years waiting too. And at last it came. A death for a death.'

She was proud of her work, but had a healthy respect for the distaste others have for a job like hers. I was the only person she'd spoken to about her previous life.

'Those cells were spotless. My girls used to take a pride in keeping their little rooms clean. Hell, they weren't really rooms, they were all open on one side. You know how they look.'

'Yes, I know how they look.' When old Janey was talking it hit me just how public was everything the condemned prisoners did. When they used their toilet bowl they were on view, and when they said their prayers. If they said prayers. The bars reminded me of an indoor zoo. Clean and sanitary, like a laboratory, but nothing to do with humans. Janey was a keeper.

'Believe me, honey, I got to be friends with practically every girl that went through. I was the closest human being to those girls that they'd had since their mothers.'

(Words are objects to me, Bobbie. With shape and colour, and sometimes with sharp corners you can feel, with smells and sounds. I thought of the way Janey used the word 'friends' about the girls on death row. When I have time I must explore what I mean.)

'I looked after them when they went through, naturally. I used to be with them when they had their wash and bring the food to them and stay while they ate. Shaved them, too. I made sure they didn't have to see themselves with too much shaved off their scalps. Just enough for the electrodes. You get close to a person when you work on their hair, when you use a blade on that person. Made me feel like a doctor sometimes. I reckon doctors must get a good feeling out of their vocation, even if there's the odd time when they know that using the knife will speed up the life process.'

She sipped her bourbon, looking back as if all her years were trees, and many dead ones still standing. I felt I really would much rather have held a long conversation with myself. I've never felt there was anything wrong in talking to oneself. However, I did the right thing at that moment, and listened to Janey.

'When it was their turn to go through, it'd be me they wanted to strap them in the chair, do up the buckles, and be there till the last moment. I'd shave their heads for the top electrode, and maybe their forearms. Some of the girls, from a life in the outdoors doing tough jobs, were quite hairy on the arms. I'd keep my voice down and whisper some of the things we used to talk about when I sat up with them at night, little jokes we had, to keep their spirits up. They appreciated it. Most women don't want others seeing they can't die quiet, like an adult woman should.'

She must have meant like a dog, Bobbie.

'They didn't want to die thinking that after they'd gone, the others would hear they were scared, and maybe even their relatives, or friends back home. No, Doc, they appreciated anything I could do to keep their spirits up. Hell, I've held their hands — like you do to the sick — until the last moment. Then I'd have to go.'

'Yes, Jane. It'd be silly getting twenty thousand volts just to be matey.'

'You said it, Doc,' she said with almost a smile. Then her face went back to concern as she switched to the process of execution.

'I had to make sure the fan was in good order, and turn it on while the legal process was in operation. We called it the legal process out of respect for the girls going through.'

'What fan?'

'Just in case,' Janey said. 'Sometimes a person actually burns. Actually, it's every time. The skin burns where the electrode touches. It was to get the smell out of the death room. It was open, Doc, there were people in the audience. It might turn them up. They might talk about it outside.'

'Is that bad?'

She was shocked. 'Doc, one breath of criticism of the way we carried out the legal process and half the jail would be out of a job. You don't understand. In a free country there gets to be a lot of criticism, not like Australia.'

'Yes, Jane. I get that part. But wouldn't it be better if the people outside the jail knew what happened when a woman gets electrocuted?'

'Are you an anti-capital-punishment freak?' she asked suspiciously.

'Well, no,' I answered. 'I don't like the electricity bit and I don't like hanging by the neck, but there are other ways I wouldn't object to. Taking a pill; or if you lost your nerve asking for an injection. With doctors in charge, like they ought to be.'

I began to elaborate, and act it up. 'A great Christmas dinner, all your friends there, a gutful of bourbon, then — pass me that bloody pill!'

She was disgusted.

'Doc, you're putting me on. There's no dignity to it like that. Why, I even had a fire extinguisher handy in case one of my friends caught fire. We wanted to do everything we could for them.'

'I still think my way's more civilised. Death's not so bad.'

'It's not supposed to be a party, Doc. These women have all killed other women or children or males and even if they haven't, that doesn't concern us, what matters is the legal process. They've all been convicted by due process. The law must take its course.'

Perhaps nothing is so ferocious or complete as the revenge of the good citizen. At all events, she said the last bit in such a savage way that I could imagine her old home town giving her the arse and telling her never to darken their bar stools again. Maybe those girls who went through didn't go through with a nice motherly picture in their minds of Janey the Jailer at all. Maybe she gloated over every moment they waited for death. Maybe they hated her guts.

Either way, she was our problem now.

Janey was one of those women you see getting old for a long time, then suddenly the process accelerates and they go downhill at speed. She had a sensible hairdo and glasses with unemphatic rims. Her gear was always clean, she loved pant-suits, but her skin looked grubby. Just that type of skin, I guess. When she went downhill, it turned grey.

She had a pension coming from the States, and nothing to do to earn it. With her girls all gone, and no one to put through, she had nothing to live for. In addition, the Supreme Court was going to make a ruling reconsidering the death penalty, a ruling that might put an axe at the roots of her existence. An axe? A bulldozer.

She went down more and more over the next few months till Christmas. Then a funny thing happened.

She got roaring drunk on beer, having abandoned her sentimental bourbon when a few shouts mistakenly included her on the edge of a big ring of drinking ladies. She usually drank alone. It was Christmas Eve, a Monday. She turned up at one of the local parties on Tuesday, and no one minded. She didn't drink much, but seemed happy to be around.

On Boxing Day, the Wednesday, she got stuck into the beer again, but with a difference. Her tongue loosened and she began to talk.

Back at the Lover's Arms round eleven in the morning, the place was full. She began to talk of the good old days and the girls and how like kin she was to the ones that had to go through and everything right up to the extractor fan that took away the smell of singeing friends from the anxious and loving but nonetheless extremely curious spectators. Really stabbing herself in the back with her own tongue.

Gradually the story gathered a crowd round her, and all sorts of intelligences were busy on the story of Janey the Jailer's social work. For a while the crowd stayed, then one by one, with maybe a shake of the head, a frown or a derisive swig and a swallow, they drifted away. Once back at their usual stations round the bar they gave a look or two back in Janey's direction, then looked away forever.

I mean forever. It was as if they all pointed the bone at her. No one from these parts of Sydney was going to turn her back on history, which went back to the first days of our little colony. And the history of a goodly number of the people of the Lover's Arms went back to the first inhabitants of the colony. And a goodly number of the early inhabitants, brothers and sisters and mothers and uncles and fathers of those inhabitants finished their existence on the end of a length of rough rope and they weren't about to drink with an executioner.

Or a trusty, a warder, or keeper. And with only very few and trusted police.

The 'tribe' at the Lover's Arms pointed the bone at Janey the Jailer by not pointing anything at her, not even their faces, and she withered away and died four months later.

Good Friday, it was.

The engineer says my memories of heaven and hell, of rogues and heroes, sanity and madness, disaster and joy, are too much for her: we are unbalanced. Yet my memories are barely enough for me! Only sixty-two and so much to remember!

Those nights when the sea like an animal brushes past me with its smell; with closed eyes I feel its breath. Its warmth seduces me and all my clothes come off. My body remembers. Oh, how my body remembers!

I dreamed last night of a valley shaped downwards like a funnel, the shape an ant-lion makes to trap ants, lying in wait at the bottom. There were rocks and trees, but no matter how I steadied myself against these natural props, my legs carried me down to the floor of the valley, shrouded in trees, to a cleared space that pointed towards the funnel's mouth. As I came near the place of danger Bobbie left me and made for the opening in the ground. Other leopards greeted her, made a fuss of her, licking her face and rubbing their heads up against all parts of her. There were hundreds more leopards in the hole, which seemed like a complicated ants' nest.

While I watched, other women slid and stumbled down the sloping sides of the valley, were seized by leopards and taken below into their nest, just as ants hoard food for winter.

Women are meat in the city of leopards.

My feet hit the pieces of a disused sign that had been torn down; faded black lettering said 'Silicon Valley'. It meant nothing to me. There were no other signs standing, though I shouldn't have been surprised to see one saying 'Valley of Leopards', or 'Funnel Valley'.

From time to time Bobbie came over and nudged me in a friendly way as if to say I would never be food for leopards. But I was uneasy at my privileged position, for more and more women were being caught and seized and hustled down into the galleries underground.

They shrieked, poor things, the air was full of cries. They knew there was no hope of avoiding their death at the teeth and claws of leopards. The shrieking and wailing woke me, and when I opened my eyes I felt guilt like a lump sitting on my chest, and I was trembling.

~

I went back to sleep praying that when she comes back, if she does, I will be here, and will still be myself.

The Pursuit of Happiness

The first rule, Bobbie, if we're going to talk about rules — and you don't, I admit, and that's what makes you a brilliant listener — is to be human. Guard your humanity. I know you understand me, better than I do. I'm talking about that girl Catto. You know, the one they used to say wasn't particular: she'd shit anywhere. Sorry for the intrusion of unpleasant matter, but you remember the last time people complained about her and she got violent and there was no outlet for her violence — for she wasn't exactly great-hearted, and could even be cowardly, if it came to that — she daubed shit on the doors of the people she was feuding with, and in the case of one place where the people had left the door open, she went inside and did some on their dining table. Removed the table cloth first, did it on the timber surface, then put the table cloth over it.

They say when she was about fifteen some males got to her, very savage ones living in the outer suburbs, and got her pregnant by blowing semen, extracted from each other, down plastic soft drink straws, into her while she was drunk.

◇

They say everyone, no matter what she's like, can be loved; whether there's any sense in doing it is another matter. I'd hesitate to apply the rule to Catto.

She was a cruel bastard. Once a year around May there's a sort of fireworks night to commemorate some triumph of defeat or empire long forgotten by the public: the sale of fireworks is the only thing keeping it going. Catto was the sort of woman — looking older than she was, never as drunk as she looked — capable of tying a firework in a dog's jaws and lighting it. Don't look at me like that, Bobbie. I bet if animals had language and more ideas, they'd be bastards like us. Or did I misinterpret your expression, darling?

I observed this heroic feat last May from the side doorway of the Conqueror's Arms. Catto lit the wick; the sparks coming from the wick alarmed the poor dog and it took off in circles. When the sparks stopped, the coloured lights came spraying out — horizontally — and when they stopped, a residual charge blew up with a bang, and its mouth blew up. This rendered the dog unconscious and took the fun out of it for Catto: she wanted to hear the dog howl and see him run like buggery.

She found another dog. She had to go to a bit of trouble to do this, since there were fireworks going off all over Sydney — kids still called them 'crackers' — and a blanket of black smoke covered the suburbs; the noise hurt the ears of dogs and they tended to hide away.

She got one, holding it by the collar, borrowed some motor oil — 20/40 multigrade, it was — and eased a roman candle into the back of the dog. She lit the wick and sent the dog up the street with a kick. Pink, blue and golden sparks spurted from the dog's rear. When it blew up after the sparks finished, Catto was satisfied. The dog flew up the street, howling and yelping.

She came into the pub.

'Oral fission was a failure, but anal fission gives a higher yield,' she commented. 'Leaves the air more shitty, though.'

I don't take to that sort of joke myself.

⇝

She spat constantly, like poor Big Jill did in her latter days. On the pub floor, grinding it into the carpet with her sandal, or outside, where she left it lie. She spat with a grimace, as if she loathed the taste of her own spit.

At work in the rubber factory, she'd hand the wrong moulds to the new girls, just for a joke, but it usually meant they didn't get their bonus. It wasn't all that funny. Those members of her audience that had not been habituated to work found it amusing enough: they didn't understand the pressures and were philosophical about the smaller pay packet, writing it off as an amusing vagary of this latest adaptation of the protean capitalist state.

I think she thought if you try hard enough and keep doing things to make you happy, you'd be successful in the end.

⇝

She'd take days off work and try to come on big as a great lover. Bev, her lover, was a dear person; quiet and loving, gentle and loyal. Quite different from Catto.

'Let's not go out into that stupid world today,' Catto would say. 'Let's pretend we're two fish in the sea; they don't have jobs to go to or houses to pay off.'

She said this when she was pretty well hung over from the night before. What she liked to think of as the laziness of love struck Bev, a much smaller girl, as the oppressions of a smelly drunk.

∽

She left Catto. Not for another woman, simply because Catto drank a lot and spat all the time.

The whole pub was surprised when Catto couldn't accept it. She drank more. For a while she'd come in exhausted just to prove she was OK for sex and didn't need sympathy. No one believed her.

Once when she was there early on a Saturday, she'd just had enough to begin to talk about herself. She latched on to me, knew I'd always listen.

'I've never been able to look at myself, sort of look inside. Bev hated me more than I'll ever know. I always think if I did look inside myself there'd be a sort of emptiness. Plenty of room. Nothing inside. You'd think there must be something in there, a scrap of this or that. But I think there'd be nothing worth looking at.' She spat.

'I don't understand,' I said.

'That's why,' she went on without answering me, 'That's why I do a few practical jokes, pull people's legs, do funny things. I don't know — life's funny. You wouldn't think she'd leave without a word. I liked her a lot.' She spat some more, she had plenty left.

∽

By six that night she was lying in the gutter outside, a little way along the street, a metre from the wheels of traffic doing their seventy-five in the sixty zone. She was lying there, still drinking, the bottle stuck up, leaning on the edge of the gutter. She got to her feet, tripped up the gutter, dropped the bottle, which broke, tried to gather the beer in her cupped hands out of the gutter, stepped carefully forward on her hands and knees and fell sideways onto the footpath.

Someone near the corner dragged her away from the edge of the road and left her.

For a few days she left the grog alone entirely, and did something about her house. It was falling to pieces. It had been modernised in such a way that it needed constant maintenance.

She thought she might have ant trouble. She'd seen ants milling around some cracks in the walls, so she ripped off a few boards from the outside. After a certain amount of destruction she found the main concentration of little black visitors, got a stirrup pump

from her shed, a bucket of Chlordane and water and sprayed like
a mad thing for fifteen minutes. She put the pump away, nailed
back the boards and went inside, triumphant. It had been a long
time since she did anything around the house; and the ants had
certainly disappeared.

But the cunning black devils had swarmed inside the house and
formed a solid wall of black on the inside of Catto's bedroom.
When she opened the door of the clothes closet she found several
million ants all over her pants and frocks and suits and the old
gowns she still had but rarely wore.

She slammed the door on the lot and went down to the pub
in disgust.

◅▻

Bev might have come back if she'd got off the alcohol, but she
wasn't up to it. She just drank herself to death. At forty-one she
had a coronary in the pub and that was that.

Some of the girls put it more kindly.

'She died of a broken heart,' they said.

*The engineer is drunk with the immensity of the world and stung by
her own smallness. Where is a god? Give me a god to swear by and I'll
swear she is a universe to me. This universe has sweet arms and oh! her
wrists! This universe has a voice that has entered my bloodstream; capil-
laries I have never seen carry that voice into the smallest recesses of my
flesh.*

But her hair. I dream her hair.

Round the corner from where I live there's a tree growing on
the edge of the footpath. This tree has been selected by the birds
of the area as a meeting place; at nightfall it is alive with birds and
birdchatter. The bitumen that grows up round its trunk is spattered
with droppings, thickly spattered. They don't care what they do it
on. There's no mistaking that this is a bird tree.

In Hyde Park, round the Archibald Fountain, there's a ring of
small-leaved fig trees — *Ficus hilli* — split by eight paths into eight
arcs. In two trees of the north-north-west arc the birds of that part
of the park gather and make a birdfuss at the same time each day.

All over the world, I guess, there are bird trees, where birds hold
meetings and have conversations and talk over the business of the
day and discuss the children; tear their relatives to bits meta-

phorically, and tell tall people-tales. And under each bird tree in the world you can find the tell-tale signs.

I should add, on second thought, that people-stories form only a small part of bird-talk.

Brain Rape

There have been more attacks on women here in the City of Women in the past few weeks. A fat lady had her thigh cut, though the attack didn't reach the sewing or raping stage, since the attacker cut the artery and the fat lady bled to death. Mary Serafini, of Cathedral Street, died of shock when her calf was opened, raped and sewn up. The mercy of an anaesthetic was denied her: she was knocked on the head. She woke during the sewing. Other victims survived; they made up a separate ward at Sydney Hospital.

The very latest was also the most brutal. Adrienne Small, nuclear psychologist, whom I had seen for labial laxness and suspected clitoral slump, was immobilised with a tranquillising dart, taken away to an old warehouse in Kent Street in the western part of the City, and there her skull was opened crudely with a hand-held power saw.

Where Adrienne was found was only horror. The warehouse walls and beams were hung with photographs of the attack, from the moment of entry of the point of the dart. The process had been interrupted a great number of times, for each time it had to be stopped — assuming one single-handed attacker — to record the progress made.

Each facet of the attack was shown: the saw tearing through hair, (no attempt was made to shave the head first and she had waist-length hair); the circular saw biting through the scalp into the bone of the skull, throwing particles of bone like sawdust; the lifting off of the rounded top of the skull, the exposure of the brain; the sight of the strong penis, the first pressure against the soft brain tissue, the probing entry, the disappearance from sight of the major portion of the shaft of the penis into the grey matter, the hairy pubis pressed against the brain case.

All this was shown in photographs from different angles, and the photos, of various sizes, hung all round. In the middle of this display — news commentators noticed its resemblance to an art exhibition — lay the body on a work bench. The first sight of it to someone coming in the door was of a pale, round expanse of brain shrouded by Adrienne's long, dark hair, pulled down in an arch on either side of the circle of penetration.

Whether she suffered, pleaded with her attacker, woke during this operation, or knew anything of it at all, can never be known; no more than you can know that the dead don't live on in some form.

It seemed to me, when I heard of it, that nothing more horribly, more plainly against women could ever be done.

Semen was found planted deep in the brain.

> *My engineer says: I want to be a ship*
> *To let the wind blow me wherever it's going,*
> *To have people sail in me to their destinations.*
> *Here I am, alive in a waste of feelings*
> *That have direction but no destination,*
> *Looking for a ship.*

There's a little lane down from Liverpool Street where small backyards are enclosed and roll-up metal shutters keep cars and yards secure. Bobbie and I walked there and saw through one open archway a brick wall covered with jasmine, the small white flowers thick against the green leaves and red-brown vines. Two children were beating the flowers with sticks; there were petals everywhere, all over the packed bricks underfoot, falling in cascades through the quiet air, sticking on their shirts, on their feet.

Two glum women watched them, occupied with their thoughts, saying nothing. Those kids were really belting shit out of that vine. We paused. They didn't seem to see us.

Usually I'd have had something to say, even if it had nothing to do with bashing flowers. This time, though the sight annoyed me, I could do nothing but repeat over and over in my head the nonsense that came into it: 'The physics of falling flowers, the physical falling of flowers, the falling of physics and flowers . . .'

Back home, movement outside my window caught my eye. At Garden Island large radar detectors turned, with that smooth clumsiness they have, tilted backwards; a network of wires turned towards the sky as if someone was expecting something to happen.

After dark, the morse flashes from a navy ship alarmed me. I don't know why. It seemed they were signalling to someone up the hill behind me, ignoring me, and I was left out. I was someone they didn't have to consider, I was someone no one had to consider.

I wasn't there.

Leopard Tears

I was reading, sitting at my window; there was a cup of coffee half-finished on the table near me, the sounds of the traffic pleasantly busy a hundred metres away and thirty below. It was a book written in the first person, on youth. I read a few pages every day; it was a book you could put down.

'Youth, Bobbie. And meaning,' I said. And began to read aloud.

We were so vacant, so free, so empty. Meaning grew, meaning that we created, but also meaning that arose in spite of us, meaning we might never understand. Meaning stranded upward out of every day, twisted together into the weave of our existence, and every day had a newness precious of itself, a newness that pointed to a future time, foreign to the past.

I continued to be strong, to run and jump and fight and play in the dirt, to romp in the grass and slide down the steep embankment carpeted with onion grass, to climb trees, wreck other kids' cubby houses in the bush, catch crayfish, dig traps for kids on overgrown bush tracks, swim in the surf, ride my horse, be late back to tea after playing streets away.

I continued to have secret conferences with my friend on her orgasm speed, to eat heartily; I learned to draw and paint and sing and play instruments and act in school plays, to throw a stone and a ball, to hurdle fences as high as my head, to swear, to ovulate, to bleed.

And I began to think.

I hadn't realised that Bobbie was no longer lying on the carpet over the other side of the room under the foxed etching in the gilt frame; I hadn't realised she'd got to her feet until there was a large paw on the open page. Her other arm came up to rest on the table, she stood on her hind legs, nearly edging me away from the book, then her head turned back towards me.

'You want to read too, darling!' I exclaimed happily.

Her head turned back to the page, her paw moved to one side, and she seemed to be looking directly at the words. I waited, to see what she would do. I waited for some time, while Bobbie looked at that page. Presently she looked away. I craned my neck around to see her face and was surprised to see a slight welling of liquid in the inner corner of the eye nearest to me.

'Bobbie!' I said. 'What's the matter? Your eyes are wet!'

Why had I been so quick to say she couldn't read? I don't know what other animals are capable of. But what could have made her eyes water? Is it possible she knows the book? If so, what is there about that poor damned and doomed girl that would excite tears? She certainly gets no sympathy from me.

'Which part has upset you, darling?' I asked.

Her right paw moved over near the middle of the page. Where the girl speaks of running and playing.

'Where's she playing?'

Bobbie looked at me and blinked slowly, the blink I take for a nod. A sort of assent.

The paw moved along.

'Playing with the other kids?'

Again the nod-type blink. And a further movement of the paw pointer.

'School and family? A family to be in? Being human and able to do all sorts of things?'

She turned towards me and put her sleek head across my shoulder so that our heads touched lightly. She allowed her head to rest there for a little while, then drew her head away and gave me an actual nod. As if she was saying 'Puss' to a cat, in an encouraging way. Two tears, one from each eye, had fallen and shone on the outer curve of her furred cheek. Gently she took herself off the table and sat by me.

◁▷

Poor ferocious creature — wildling out of place — trapped in a City of Women.

A shower of rain drifted across from the harbour and, as I watched, it began to rain in William Street. The bitumen was delighted, steaming and pleased, freshened by the fine drops.

In a few minutes I could smell it. I love the smell of fresh showers on warm bitumen.

My wise engineer insists it is best to know, but always to consider there is so much more to know, that you know nothing.
That's it: fight me with words.
Where is a word for the way she gets up from a chair, or sits down? Give me one word for the fine skin that scarcely veils the veins of her breasts.

I have a little iron handle with a square hole in one end; I use it to get water for Bobbie in the different parks we visit. Its hole fits over the square spindles on park taps, which have no handles.

I make a pool of water and Bobbie laps it up.

Last night as we walked in the dark Domain, I did my water trick and as Bobbie drank I stood and looked up at the magnificent buttery full moon as it rose, floating above the Hyatt Kingsgate building at the top of William Street.

'Shine on Bobbie, you cheerful fat moon,' I said.

Four-footed Bobbie looked up from drinking; at me then at the moon. Her eyes shone strangely. Enough to make me shiver, and not know why. I think, sometimes, I get afraid too easily. But maybe I'm not myself today. And the reason? Because I'm Bobbie . . .

◁▷

If I could, just once more, listen at her ear-shells and hear the tide of her memory.

The Harmless Games of Old Women

In Hyde Park, old women like gasping drowners, walking forward behind their outstretched grasping knuckles; washing their teeth under the bubblers, spitting a mugful on the asphalt, head in hands — one poor thing afflicted with a face reminiscent of the aged George Bernard Shaw, another's like the condemned-cell photograph of Hermann Goering — such red faces and white; such grey countenances; such greeny-yellowy not-long-for-this-world old ladies; the whiskers untrimmed though sparse like those of elderly Asian men; the white spittle; the fascinated and appalled city women, smart and shining, not a caries in the world (couldn't resist it) passing by on business, shaking their heads over the brown wine bottles on the public grass, looking away when the wreckage of humanity and the shrivelled hopes of youth speak to them and point and begin some impossible story they have no ending for; the sailors stepping on to the park grass uncomfortable at the contrast they see between the tenuously living and the emphatically healthy; the sunken garden tiered with domestic flowers regular and complacent and proud in full beauty; the gardeners cutting the grass under foreign ornamented trees, and disturbing soil near the sea-monster roots of derided Moreton Bay figs; the Russian sadness and native absurdity of the wet statuary in the fountain and Apollo hung with the penis of a nine-year-old boy.

The world looks like a soiled handkerchief here. Bright lunchtime girls move in a dream far from their minds; the trees move, all moves out of step with the foot-in-the-grave old women, who, caught for an instant still, hold the sun immobile in their fierce, dim eyes.

One has a certain grace about her withered mouth, just at the corners; you have to look carefully to see it. The beauty of a young girl has not been entirely wiped away; it's gone in places but at the corners it clings. Harshness, the seasons, loss, the bitterness of memory, the reckoning of time, have not won yet.

Funny old ladies with cross-over toes are making a game of catching a man with a net; the man is played by the shabbiest, smallest one; she tries not to evade the net. Along with all their torsions, abatements and declines, they laugh uncontrollably. The truth will set you free, I want to say to them, or some such foolishness, but it means nothing, words mean nothing, no more than their game means.

One, who looks like a clown — merry with it, too — is eating; she takes a long time, chewing on naked gums, to get through her sandwich.

They are all laughing at once. Who can help them?

To help the poor you need to have something to give.

◁▷

Comfortable women when they retire play gardeners or grandmothers or drunks or tourists or trippers or fisherwomen or sundials. Some choose to play toy soldiers. Retired service officers, retired chairwomen of boards, retired directors of companies, retired managers of many kinds join the new organisation, Senior Service, to amuse themselves, to belong among their kind, to provide a back-up force in the event of a law-and-order breakdown: to restore society when it falls sick — still afraid of a socialism that is one of the many guises of capitalism.

Most of the time their manoeuvres are harmless, though under the influence of financial sadness or property anxiety they make mistakes which have to be hushed up by powerful friends. I can be no more specific, Bobbie, for fear of the repressive harshness of our laws.

The respectable poor do not resemble the rich in their range of activities. They sit on patios and talk to children, telling as stories the memories they've accumulated. Ruined as old rugs, as old tired pets. Ruined as an old bay that was once good for kids to swim in and paddle their boats out over the shallowed water, that's now reclaimed for other purposes. Or as a bay that's been laid waste, that is now dried mud and the water is reluctant to come there; old memories minus their labels are half-buried in the discoloured sand, and the place stinks, and it's dying.

◁▷

The last game for the lot of them is not a revival of hoops or hopscotch or any other thing: the last game is falling asleep and playing dead.

◁▷

Coming across the grass by Elizabeth Street is a young girl in singlet and shorts on a red tractor drawing three gangs of mowers, which send a cascade of grass high behind their flashing blades.

Like me, Bobbie can smell the cut grass; we both lift our heads to catch the full sweetness of it.

My young engineer imagines she is as great as the boundless universe, and I agree. I wish she'd be satisfied with that, and come back.

The peach stone I planted in one of the large pots on the roof, that became a young tree, has miraculously come into bloom. Pink peach blossoms are cupped open on every one of the twelve branches; there are seventeen flowers on the biggest. Their perfume is very faint, but their warm colour leaps to the eye among the other poor potted spiky plants that have to struggle so hard to stay alive.

How did this happen? How could a tree, grown in a pot, so far from others of its kind, burst into carefree, beautiful bloom?

Why did it happen? There was no future here. There was no one going to plant it out in an orchard or backyard. It would exhaust the fuel in the soil it had, then die.

It makes me shiver when I think how brutal the circumstances were that arranged for such hope, such beauty, such radiant youth to be spent on a poor living thing that *must* die before it can reach a proper age. But I was the circumstances; I planted it: I am responsible.

I felt that if it must die, I could not allow it to die alone. I man-handled the pot over to the back lift and brought it down off the roof to my place, one floor below. There was enough dying in the world, and quite enough unhappiness. Never enough of loveliness.

The branches and blossoms look a picture, over against my white wall. It is a great comfort having it with me.

But wait! That pink and white! Last time I saw Ivy, standing under the red glow of the tavern lights, her face had the same pink bloom on white skin under black hair and brows. After the life she'd had!

It's a great comfort having a thought like that.

Music that Talks to Machines

I'd walked such a long way with Bobbie, I was so tired. I found myself a long way out of the City on the safer, southern side, among people I didn't want to look at or know. I needed a lift home.

He didn't recognise me. The car that pulled up had Gordon at the wheel, my Gordon from years ago. I'm sure he didn't recognise me. Have I changed so much? Poor Gordon. He tried to be a good husband, but my work was my husband and my master: he must have felt lost when I sent him away. He must have felt I was ruthless. Bobbie had graduated; she and I would be together forever.

He drove, I stared out of the car window.

As we got closer to the City, a funny thing happened: the streets began to change. I thought I knew them, but when I looked more closely I found they weren't like anything I'd seen. They began to be fewer and fewer, until it was countryside all round. And about the time we should have been back in the middle of my much-loved City we'd climbed a big hill on to a high ridge, and looked down into a wide, round valley. Funnel Valley, of course. Right at the bottom in the centre was the cleared space where I remembered — from my dream a few letters back — the opening in the ground. From the ridge it looked like a place people lived.

Gordon stopped the car and looked. His eyes were hard with long sorrow. He hadn't changed all that much, just looked a lot older. I'm older, too. Why aren't I wise?

'I never knew this settlement was here,' he said, and shook his head. Admiringly, I'd say. Did he think I lived here?

'I didn't think the Western Valley Road went as far as this.'

Western Valley Road? Where did he think he was? Was he dreaming?

He looked round, the road swept like a skirt below us, entering the valley in a corkscrew motion at a shallow angle. The colour of a roof here and there on the way down could be seen through treetops, but the shroud of trees was too thick to allow a better view of the buildings or even the road as it screwed down into the narrowing valley. Some trees were steel-grey, brittle as bone.

'A good view,' he granted.

What he meant was trees. We had trees all right, plenty; it was food we lacked. (I did live here, of course I did.) You can't eat gum leaves, turpentine, sassafras, bloodwood, oak.

'When I retire,' he said. 'A place like this. Maybe some water, a creek, or near the sea.' He sounded glad to talk of old age, retiring.

On the way down into the valley he took an interest in all he saw: waterfalls, vegetable clearings, fruit trees, carpet-like lawns, buildings clean and neat and silent, and in what he didn't see: people.

'There's no one in the streets. That's funny.'

Suddenly he said, 'The town's dead.'

It was hardly a town, but I didn't want to argue. He was kind, giving me a lift on my way, so far from home.

'No animals either,' he discovered. But whether he was pleased I couldn't tell.

We were home. Bobbie and I got out. He looked at the money I offered him and said no, but he was pleased I offered.

'Keep to the low side for the road out,' I said. 'You can't miss.'

His car moved off along the road, scrunching gravel; people came from every house he passed, stood and watched him go round and round in our valley of women with the steep sides like an ant lion's pit.

When it was dark we would see his lights like snail's horns feeling for a way, his car slower in tighter circles; he would be tired, confused.

No animals, he said. We keep animals in cages; he couldn't know how scarce food was in isolated settlements, or how your mouth could water for cooked flesh. Gordon would be knocked on the head and cleaned, would be divided, to each house a share. Soon Ailsa the crane driver would drop his car and belongings down Deepwater Hole.

There are cheerful voices now and kids are on the street.

They always know when I bring home some meat.

◁▷

I stumbled and fell, my face against the base of a tree. Was it a bottle tree? I came to myself looking up at Bobbie. Meat? I? What was I doing? What had happened? I was just as much a stranger to this valley as Gordon was. What was this place doing to me? Deepwater Hole? What was that?

This was Funnel Valley, there were leopards down there. There was no Gordon any more, no car, no houses, no road: just a steep valley, rocks and trees and undergrowth. The steepness pulled me down, Bobbie sprang lightly between the rocks, we were on the floor of the valley in no time.

Over near the hole in the earth leopards were climbing out, leopards were jumping down out of sight like a mess of ants tumbling together, so many there was no sense to their coming and going, so many you couldn't see if they were just repeating the same actions over and over, giving the impression of large numbers and designed, or senseless, activity.

Closer to the hole Bobbie and I went, until I could see down there all the machines; smooth rows of machines, a whole city of them, rank on rank, file after file, making little noise except a quiet contented hum. With illuminated faces and small green, red and orange lights and musical sounds — cheeky little beeps and cheep-cheeps: the sort of music that talks to machines — above the continual hum.

I thought of battery chicks. Where were the hens to which those machines were chicks? Where were the minds behind the machines?

I saw struggling, protesting women brought by leopards near the machines, and a kind of arm from the machines passed in front of the human faces as if wiping them clean. After this, their struggles ceased; the women became limp, like meat.

Fear, like tight brittle glass, held me all over.

Then I saw the leopards, instead of moving fluidly and with smooth grace, moved jerkily, like clockwork. Did the machines tell them what to do? They took the limp human meat away from the lines of machines, to another part of the underground city.

One leopard moved too close to the machine arms, which wiped across its face, after which it fell to the floor like a bag of loose things. Others removed it.

'All flesh is meat in the city of machines,' I said to Bobbie, and put out my hand to her, half to steady myself.

My hand encountered nothing. I looked down to find her. Bobbie was far below.

My head wobbled. I was dizzy. I seemed to be shooting high into the air. I didn't even have to flap my arms to make flying movements like I do in dreams.

Already the figures on the ground were tiny mites, the valley diminishing, its borders pulling in quickly until it was a round, shaded hole in the surrounding country. Which was a light tan colour, like a young woman's belly.

In fact, it *was* a belly.

Higher and higher. The breasts came into view, the head bent forward, the mouth opening and closing: she was singing. Her legs stretched away into the distance under water.

My own, real, first and only Bobbie was lying on the sand of a beach, waves came in and rolled gently over her; water stayed in pools on her surfaces, people paddled in the shallows, a line of people on holidays hand in hand paddled happily, splashing and kicking up spray, walking towards me down a gentle slope from her belly to her waist.

Her navel — its tiny precipitous sides plunging towards darkness and the entrance to another world — was now submerged. Shells sang, starfish whirled slowly round, blue-domed crabs marched in ranks; in deeper waters sharks sped.

To them she was the land, the solid earth that underlies the visible world.

The sea lapped her limbs, salt water pooled again on her chest, swirled round the hills of her naked breasts. They looked such feeble waves, to be cooling her surfaces. But what of the vast interior, the dynamic, hot recesses of her workings — the chasms, fissures, crevasses? What tides pulled there?

∽

I call to her from a great distance. She makes no answer, but goes on singing.

Am I a shadow?

The clouds here are low. I put up my hand, I feel their touch as my hand passes through them. Cool and moist.

Am I as substantial as a shadow? Am I merely an echo bounced off the events of my lived life?

Perhaps for me all time has already happened and my existence is a memory. Perhaps all of us are memory come alive; through us time is remembered, ghosts playing a recording of human life over and over, the memories of lost races.

What a mouthful. Perhaps it's no such thing.

∽

I'm sure it was all a dream. Unlike most I have, this one hasn't faded. Still I see her, huge as a beach, waves washing her, people paddling in her shallows, her head bent forward, the strange sounds of her singing tuneless as the sea. And the valley, the distressed women, the clockwork leopards, the machines — all are drowned under the waves of the sea and so tiny in scale it seems inconceivable I was ever there.

❧

I turn to my peach tree. Its petals speak to me across the still air of my white, sun-filled room. There are little knobby lumps that soon will unclench and open out into fingers of leaf. While I watch, a petal falls to the green carpet. I must have shaken it loose, bringing it down from the roof.

How absurd that I, an old tree, should be stirred by a spring. Next thing I'll be in bloom, putting out fists of leaves to catch the sun.

My beautiful engineer must turn like a leaf
To catch the full sun and the rain
Before it is her time to grow yellow
And drop off the tree.

Such a disturbance in the corridor this afternoon!

I was having my rest and thinking happily of my two Bobbies. I didn't want to be forced to think of other people's troubles and rather resented their noise. I didn't even bother to get up off my bed and walk to the front door; I just wanted to do what *I* wanted: to be undisturbed and think my own thoughts, and when *I* wanted to go out and seek the company of others, I would.

I couldn't help hearing the voice of some young woman clamouring for her mother to open the door. I expect it must have been the apartment opposite.

'Please, mother!' I heard her say. 'Please open the door! It's me!' And the knocking followed, rather sharp knock-knock-knocks, yet not loud enough to be alarming to her mother if she suffered from nerves or was in any way ill.

The caretaker was with her. She answered something the young woman said by saying, 'No, she hasn't been out for some time. She never goes out. She had some big love affair, and it ended; and she came here.'

My peach tree has dropped more petals. I suppose it's only to be expected, being shut in. From my bed I can see it beside the coffee table. And a parallelogram of sun on the carpet. Light defines itself by what isn't light, doesn't it?

'Not for months,' the caretaker repeated. She *would* repeat things if you didn't interrupt.

'It's been ages. The other person went away and left her. Then she came here.'

My darling Bobbie, an empty room is the reality I face, nevertheless I wish you many years in the warm sun of life. How you looked when you said: 'Every minute must be packed, saved and packed.'

'Hasn't left the room since her cat died. A big yellowy thing, it was. Bigger than ordinary cats. Used to take it round on a lead. Reminded me of a wild animal, I thought it might be a Tasmanian devil. It wouldn't have anything to do with anyone but her.'

Poor woman. Such a dumb and dangerous pet for a decaying mother.

Then an alarming thing happened. A man's voice said, 'How d'you know she's in there?'

A male, in the City of Women!

Why hadn't they caught him? How did he get through our defences? Were they asleep on the Edge of the City?

Surrounded by light, in its degrees, a form of darkness gripped me, my mind struggled in panic. I didn't want darkness yet.

'She pays her maintenance every month on the dot,' the caretaker said. 'Also, I hear the dishes being washed, I smell cooking, coffee on the stove, the television on. She's there, all right. Besides, she writes letters all the time. I post them. I have a lot of letters to post from this building. There's a lot of sick people never get out, you know.'

'Why won't she answer?' said the man.

'How would I know? All I know is, I never have any trouble with her, she's always good as gold. She has her shopping brought up once a week, why don't you come then? Fridays. Are you sure you know her?' Then a pause. The caretaker didn't seem at all terrified, and, evidently satisfied they meant no harm, washed her hands of the whole thing and went away. But how did a man get past the Edge of the City? Men are meat . . . I had a feeling of being lost, yet I knew the forest I was lost in wasn't real.

'Mother, please open the door!' the young woman called. 'I just want to see that you're all right! Please talk to me! Just say hullo.'

Strange how little going on means, when the one who gives it meaning goes. I wonder if she's changed. But of course she has. I wonder how much.

'Tell her I'm here,' said the man. 'She's never met me.'

Live on, my darling, my baby. At sixty-two I haven't twenty years to live, but what I remember of you will die only when I die.

'She's funny about men. Didn't even go to father's funeral. You stand out of the way, round the corner.'

'If she doesn't want to see us, let's go,' said the man. 'Write her another letter and put the address in big letters so she doesn't go sending it up the coast.'

I couldn't help listening to what they were saying, but how I wished they'd go.

My Bobbie, I wanted to hold you tight, and I did. Too tight, it seems. When you were born I held you. That wasn't too tight, was it?

'I just want to see that she's all right. I wish she hadn't taken it so hard that I didn't love the work as much as she did, and didn't put up a fight when I had to go. I wish she'd been content, with me at least qualifying and working with her. It's no one's fault that the new software phased me out. She shouldn't have built up her hopes so much. You can't count on passing jobs from parent to child any more.'

'She wanted you to carry on where she left off, to live her life through you. You've decided you want a family as well as a profession. Something's got to give.'

My Bobbie, what has moulded my love to this shape? Time causes ruins; time rots things as surely as if it were acid: time is to blame.

'I can go back to engineering. She always wanted me to be a consultant — thought there was safety in that . . . I hope she's all right.'

What did she mean: engineering? What sort of engineer was she? But I gave this nothing more than the ragged end of my thought; I was happy to lie still and to be moved by my Bobbie's distant music, the music that she is.

'Call round again tomorrow,' the man said. 'Bring the doctor. Women can't resist doctors. She's bound to have something a doctor can fix.'

With me, it's different. Instead of sicknesses and cancers and a failing heart, I go forward from day to day, healthy into sorrow.

'She hates doctors. Thinks they're unnecessary.'

'She's not sick, is she?'

'Don't talk like that about mother,' the young woman said calmly. 'She's perfectly all right, for her age.'

I'll never surrender to what has happened, sooner the pain than say it's all for the best. It's not for my best. I won't accept rejection. I don't believe in self-sacrifice. I don't see how self-sacrifice is any sort of fulfilment. Self-denial is no form of self-expression for me.

'Maybe she ought to be in a home.'

Hopes can become broken glass; you can be standing among them.

'I'm worried about her. All alone.'

Her soul was clear as a rock pool that God put by the sea to remind him of how beautiful things were that he'd made.

'Come on, let's go. She'll live forever.'

I heard them clearly, but I was trying to think. I was wrong about Bobbie doing languages at school, and it hurts me now that I was so wrong. I'm glad she went against me. Yet I made her for myself; she will never be at rest till she comes back to rest in me.

'She tried to keep you tied to her dream-strings. Always something wrong with her. Made up half her ailments.'

I can see her face, that clear soul looking out at me — direct, honest, wiser than I.

'She was always about to die, but you'd get old, waiting. She's a tough old stick. She'll manage. In a few years time we'll have her out to our place, playing with the kids.'

'Years! Do you really think so?'

'Sure I do. You've been under her thumb long enough. When she sees there's nothing she can do, no amount of pressure will stop you, she'll come round. This is a passing thing. She had to overcome a lot to break into her field, she's still as strong as she was. She hated to have to retire. It'll be a fight.'

I remember waiting for her, years ago, waiting for her to come. It was always going to be wonderful, and it was. Even the birth was wonderful. For years I'd been empty, so empty, not really knowing who I was — I'd done what I wanted, become an engineer, but I wanted more — until she came. I'm still full of her, as if not all of her has been born.

The young woman in the corridor said loudly, 'Mother, let go!'

My skeleton wears flesh to feel the press of her kisses on. But motion is all: there is no rest, no peace, until everything stops.

I was glad when they went away from there and the fuss finished, glad they took their troubles with them. But I was sorry for the mother, and wished her luck in coping. She must have been lonely, too. At least I know I've won a little from life, having loved.

But to think of it — men in our City!

Just to make sure, I got up and went to my window. For a few seconds I was shaken. The solemn building fronts looked straight ahead and down, in meditation, but it seemed to me that our City of Women had vanished and the streets were back as they once were: men everywhere, just as many as women; men sweeping the streets, men watering grass in the park, men driving cabs, men sitting in the gutter, men's voices in the street below me, men talking with women — the whole box and dice.

But there was a difference. All was decay. The males moved sluggishly, their faces seemed to *flow*, there were holes on their surfaces, like bomb craters on a landscape, their flesh crawled. The buildings swayed, as if turned to a heavy sludge only just solid enough to stay upright. The grass in the park ebbed and flowed, the bitumen road creased and wrinkled. As I watched, cars and trucks slowed and began to solidify, becoming one with the road, their drivers and passengers melting into the vehicles.

The world out there was huge and terrifying — and more ugly than I'd ever seen it. As I watched, it began to pour in through my window like an avalanche, filling my familiar space with smells of volcanoes and putrefaction; with awkward, unwanted shapes and masses, crunching and squelching up against one another, grinding and slipping against the walls, threatening to destroy my world and bring down everything; pushing me, crushing me, trying to alter me, trying to eliminate me, to stamp me out forever separate from my love.

I shut my eyes tight to dismiss this invasion, and was relieved to have the universe instantly obey my wishes, to hear the unmistakable rushing sound of my room clearing, emptying of this frightening world. When I opened my eyes, the world was outside, in its proper place. I shut the windows quickly. But males were still in sight down below.

I was in a nightmare.

I tried to shout, but my voice died. The shut windows laughed at me. There was no one to call, anyway, and no one would ever understand. Could I signal some other way? How? To whom? But there was no need. All, all I saw down there were turned to me, pointing. I stepped back, away from the window, grabbing for a curtain to pull across. No curtain; I had abolished curtains. I had wanted there to be nothing between me and the world. I wish I'd been ill and had restored the curtains.

Eyes. It was my eyes had done this to me. Only my eyes could have pictured the outside world heavy as sludge, moving objects solidifying, live things rotting yet not dying.

The sun was merciless, pushing down. I went to the casement and looked out. The pointing had stopped, people were moving. Shadows everywhere, though, were heavy, pulling the buildings over; human figures, too, leaned into the sun, dragging their shadows' counterweights.

I blinked hard again and again, squeezing the muscles of my eyelids down hard, feeling my cheeks pushing up to help. I opened my lids, just a slit, several times, to make sure I was focussing correctly, then when I looked again with wide open eyes the world was normal . . .

Of course. I was so suggestible. Alarm had made me see things that weren't there. I calmed down and looked round, in the dear dear sun that warms me, at the familiar view of city skyline, Domain, harbour, Woolloomooloo, with all my usual affection beaming out on my loved City of Women (the city of women is love), and north — so far north! — to that heaven on the coast where my Bobbie is.

✑

I'll never let go.

✑

It was good that the world was its usual self. I found I'd been crying a little, my cheeks were wet. Obviously, there's more to tears than grieving. I resolved to buck up, endure what I have to endure, and not to talk of love.

✑

Perhaps she can't be completely born until I'm dead.

✑

I started to write this letter.

I daresay I'll go for a walk with Bobbie to post it, perhaps even find myself in Cathedral Street and stop for a while at the Lover's Arms. Yes, and drink too much again.

(If only the stairs to heaven stretched further than Cathedral Street.)